Idle,

Wild,

Love

Shaida Escoffery

Printed in the United States of America

First Printing, 2013

ISBN-13 **978-0615921402**

ISBN-10: **061592140X**
KRSD Books
Miami, FL

www.shaidaescoffery.com

Have mercy upon me, O God, according to thy lovingkindness: according unto the multitude of thy tender mercies blot out my transgressions.

Wash me throughly from mine iniquity, and cleanse me from my sin.

For I acknowledge my transgressions: and my sin is ever

before me.

Psalm 51:1-3

Where the Men are IDLE

<u>Henry</u>

1924

A warm summer breeze blew around them as they dug into the brown earth, their fingernails turning the same color as their skin. They were burying their hearts in the dirt. Both of their fathers had died in the Great War and their mothers had moved them up here to Idlewild, Michigan. Both mothers weren't prepared for the coolness of the place. The air so clear, they wanted to breathe in lungfuls of it. Each sunrise brought a promise of a fresh start and separation from Jim Crow. Each sunset signaled success. They had moved in next door to each other and their mothers had clung together for support, talking each day for hours after work. They soon followed suit. Whenever their mothers were at work they walked home from school, playing all day before they noticed the setting sun. They would rush home, sweeping floors, straightening beds, and dusting. But it never was a big deal because their mothers would come home exhausted, until one of them would call out through the window, and then the two families would meet together for dinner.

They had made ceramic hearts in their class at school. Everyone had been so excited because they never thought a Negro school would have enough money to make things out of ceramic. But their teacher, Mrs. Henderson had wanted them to have a well-rounded education, learning everything from science to art to music, even if they were only eight. Henry said they should bury those hearts in the dirt, and when they got older they would dig them back up.

"Wait," Hannah said, holding Henry's arm with her dirty one. "I don't think we should bury them."

"Why not?" Henry said, stopping.

"Why did you think we should bury them?"

"Cause my daddy always used to talk about how he buried a box of letters he had for my mama, and when he asked her to marry him, he dug'em back up. So we can bury this and when I ask you to marry me, then we'll dig'em back up."

"Why you want to marry me?"

Henry shrugged. "I don't know. You're the only one it would make sense to."

And so they buried those hearts and forgot about them.

Hannah wasn't a very pretty girl and Henry knew that. But, they were friends, so he stuck by her. Henry was handsome. So handsome that more and more he was finding himself having to turn down girls because he was stuck with Hannah. He was sixteen, and he was strapped down to this girl like she was his wife. There were girls with shapely breasts, wide hips, and round bottoms. Then there was Hannah with her nappy hair and small breasts that looked even smaller under those clothes her mother made her wear. He hadn't told Hannah, but he'd kissed Maureen Collins one day behind school. Her kiss had felt better than Hannah's had. Hannah had been too nervous and tense and only made the kiss last a second before she drew away, embarrassed and ready to go home. Maureen let their lips settle together before

Henry could do whatever he wanted with her. He knew he had to be with her. He had his boys tell Maureen that he wanted her to be his girl and the next day he and Maureen were hand in hand, walking the whole 17 miles to Reed City where all the Negroes had to go to school after the sixth grade. Hannah came to him that day during school before they went to their arithmetic class.

"Is Maureen your girl?"

"Yeah," Henry said, awkwardly as he watched Hannah's fingers fidget with her notebook.

Her voice shook a little, and she looked down as she spoke. "I thought I was your girl."

He looked around before pulling Hannah to the side where no one could see. "Hannah, it's just that Maureen is...more my type of girl."

Something flashed in Hannah's eyes as she looked up at him. "Pretty. She's pretty."

"Yeah, and I really like her."

"And I'm not?"

"Hannah, you don't have to make it sound like that."

"But it's the truth isn't it?"

"Hannah we're best friends, just not anything like that." He said, holding her arm.

She pulled her arm away. "We're not friends either."

June 1940

The sound of the steam train at the Pere Marquette Railroad stop, as well as the ash that shot out from the top of it, was overwhelming. Henry closed his eyes tight at the sound of the train. It reminded him of the days he'd have to run home when they lived in Mississippi to avoid running into some white boys looking to torture some poor nigger. When he was young he'd have to run along the train tracks to get home, and the sound of the trains close by would heighten his terror. There were people bustling all around the station, their suitcases and trunks piled on top of one another as they waited for taxis. It was summer, and in Idlewild that meant tourists. You could hear them from when they hit Baldwin. There were colored doctors, lawyers, businessmen, and their families with them, all avoiding the segregation of the hotels in the major cities. The stations were all wooden built, and still not too shabby considering they'd been built a little before Henry and his mama had moved up here, fleeing Mississippi. Henry's mom and Mrs. Evans had sent him out here to pick up Hannah while they stayed back and prepared a feast for her. He'd read all the news reports about the trouble brewing in Europe and agreed with Mrs. Evans that Hannah should come home. But, shoot, he didn't get that much extra attention when he came back from college. But, Hannah was some poster child, cause she went off to France to be a governess. It made him chuckle each time he thought of Hannah in her ill fitting dresses walking around Europe. Man, the last time he had seen Hannah had been the day of graduation. Well, technically it was the night of graduation. He had been sneaking out the window after spending the night with a girl in her dormitory. Hannah had been walking to the bathroom. She hadn't said a word, just only stared at him with disdain before turning away. Henry now looked at his watch, it wasn't anything fancy, it didn't even have a brand name. It was simple watch with a white face and with a black leather band. It had been a gift from his mother when he'd gone off to college.

Her train should've come in by now. He wasn't going to wait all day out here for her. He looked around spotting a sweet looking girl with mahogany skin sitting on a bench nearby. Maybe he could make this trip worthwhile after all.

"Hey, pretty lady," he said, taking off his hat and flashing her a smile.

"Henry?" she said.

"You know me?" Henry said, stunned.

"Yeah," she said, smiling. "I take it you don't remember me."

"I don't think we've met," Henry said, sitting next to her.

She smiled and Henry thought about how good it would feel when he kissed those lips. Oh, he would have fun with her.

"Oh, I think we have," she said.

"I would've remembered a face as pretty as yours." She'd come alone so maybe she was like one of those girls who had come up here two years ago, interviewing to be nurses. The men here went crazy with the influx of women here for about three months straight. He'd had his fill of so many of them that to be honest the names and faces blended into one another sometimes. Or maybe she was up here to meet a lover or had a rich husband or daddy around. But as he looked at the brown eyes haloed by sweeping lashes, recognition set in. He stilled and once again looked at her mouth that had that tiny cleft on her bottom lip, before confirming it with his words.

"Hannah?"

She scoffed at him. "You haven't changed one bit. Still a Casanova."

Henry smiled. "No, but I've got a charm, you must admit."

"I guess certain women might find you charming."

"And you don't?"

She rolled her eyes and shook her head.

"Well, I'm sure I'll change your mind."

"What makes you think that?"

Henry smirked. "Trust me. I don't think you'll last until the end of the summer."

Hannah scowled and sat back against the bench. Her pink dress fit her well. "You're so arrogant. I suppose that hasn't changed either."

"You know me too well," Henry said, knowing his sarcasm would tick her off. They both sat there watching the other passengers greeting family and friends across the platform. "I suppose I'll take your bags to the car now." He started to pick up her suitcases. Geez, how much stuff had she brought from Paris?

"I don't want to go with you."

"What?" He said, turning around to face her.

"I said; I'm not going with you. I'll find someone else to carry me home."

"And just who the hell do you think will carry you home?" Henry said.

"I'll get a driver. I'll figure my way out."

Hannah might have changed looks, but she was still stubborn as a mule. Henry sighed and put her bags back down. "Fine. Get home by yourself. It's a long walk in case you don't remember."

She stood up now and met his eyes. "Yes, I remember. Don't worry, I'll find a driver."

Henry looked around for a driver but didn't see anyone.

"No need to wait around for me. I'm sure you have better things to do with your time. Perhaps you should look about changing another girl's mind."

He tipped off his hat to her. "Alright Hannah, I'll see you later." He started to walk away before turning back to say, "And just to let you know, I have changed the mind of every woman in town already." He winked at her and watched her glare at him before walking off to his 1939 Plymouth coupe.

Henry got to his car, but decided to wait until she had gotten a driver before leaving. He waited about ten minutes, watching her drag her four suitcases before he saw a worker help her, and then arrange a taxi ride for her. That guy probably thought she was loaded like all the vacationers, especially with all those bags. He shook his head the whole time. Stubborn woman. He decided he would just go to Pete's for a while before heading over to Mrs. Evan's house. Pete's was his favorite place, with its wooden structure painted green, attracting people to its nightlife.

It wasn't very large, but then again most places weren't large, except maybe the Flamingo and Paradise Club. So, each night it was packed with people dancing and drinking. Sometimes they had to send people out because it was too crowded. Henry came so often that he and Pete had become friends and Pete always let him drink free because when he got loose, he was always able to bring in customers and keep them there for hours.

He entered the old bar, its insides dark because most of the windows were right by a tree that blocked out the light. There was a small wooden stage, that needed fixing every few days from the dancers ruining it. Pete had to buff the floors every three days.

Pete called out to him. "Hey, my man! You a little early ain't ya?" Pete stood around the bar, cleaning glasses, his grey hair mixing with the black. Pete was a stout dark-skinned man and Henry stood almost a head over him. He always complained that his gut never came from the liquor he sold, in fact, he barely drank. He wouldn't want to waste any of his profits. But, it was those damned salted peanuts he kept in a dish at the bar. He was always munching on them and as a result, retaining water weight.

"Yeah, I wasted my day waiting at the train station."

"For what?"

"You remember Hannah Evans?"

"Yeah sure."

"Well, she's came back from France."

"I still can't picture Hannah in a place like France," he said, as he poured Henry a glass of scotch.

Henry laughed as he took his glass. "Neither can I. Hannah wouldn't even fix her hair." He decided to not tell Pete yet how Hannah didn't look like the same person they both remembered.

"I heard them Frenchies love them some colored people," he said, stroking his goatee. "Imagine if we went to France? We'd have women every night."

"I ain't short of that here. But that don't sound too bad," Henry said, taking a drink.

"You think Hannah's been with some white men there?"

Now, Henry really laughed. "No man here wanted Hannah. What makes you think that some white man would want her? Plus, you know Hannah's all about church."

"True."

Henry drank the rest of the scotch and handed the empty glass back to Pete. "Alright, well I won't be in tonight. Gotta stay for dinner."

"Alright Henry, see you later," Pete called, as Henry headed out the club. Henry drove along the unpaved road, thinking back to the days at Howard when he was getting a degree in architecture. What a waste. Here he was in Idlewild, the Negro's haven and he couldn't get a job. Cause at the end of the day, white people ran everything and controlled who got a job, even if they didn't live in the dang town. It didn't matter if he got an education and could probably build a house better than them. All they saw was his skin. So, when the summer was up and all them rich folks went back to wherever they came from, he was stuck working construction in

Baldwin or in Reed City for people that paid him close to nothing, and called him a nigger.

He drove along the tree-lined pathway and pulled up to the house with its old wood that creaked and needed a fresh coat of terracotta colored paint. Both of their houses were a bit strange in that they were some of the few two story houses. There were very few residents in Idlewild year round. The residents were middle class or lower so it wasn't uncommon for them to just have a small wooden house, just like the vacation houses the rich tourists had. They called them doghouses around here. Mrs. Evans and Henry's mama had blown most of their savings, paying for men to build them two story houses with a porch so that they could give their children an experience unlike the South. It was a bad choice: those porches. They only collected snow that Henry had to go out and shovel all the time in the winter. The only thing they hadn't done was splurge to buy property on the lake. But, the men had been sloppy in their construction and Henry had spent all his teenage years fixing a plank here and there in both houses. It was where he'd become so fascinated with architecture, watching the men across the lake build these new hotels and houses, and wondering when he'd get to do the same. His mama wanted him to fix up Mrs. Evans house, as well as their own next door. But he would always tell her that he'd get around to it. Now, he was too busy making cabins and big houses around Lake Idlewild and Paradise Lake for the rich Negroes; or having to travel to other cities in Michigan to get picked for work to build some family's second home.

He opened the door to the house yelling that he was here. His mama had him paint the whole house in white, saying she could pick any furniture to go with it. He'd complained, but she'd insisted, although she didn't have a lot of money for the furniture to make the inside look nice. She just bought whatever she could afford. So, the house lay arrayed with random colored furniture. A yellow couch, red cushioned chair with a blue rug. All against those white walls that had to be repainted every couple years because it grew dingy. The only positive feature to opening his front door was that the smell of fresh baked bread that always met him. He rounded the corner to see the three women sitting at the dining table, fortunately, the only furniture that his mom had gotten as a set.

"Hannah ended up taking a taxi here," Mrs. Carrington said. "Henry, I told you to get Hannah at the train station."

"Mrs. Rosie, I decided to come on my own. I knew that Henry has a busy schedule and I figured I'd save him the trouble," Hannah said.

"I thought you said your day was free Henry?" Mrs. Evans asked, bringing out the rest of food to the table that had been weathered by time.

Henry cleared his throat taking the open seat next to Hannah. "It was. Hannah shouldn't have assumed."

Hannah slyly looked over to Henry. "I'm sorry for the assumption."

He shot her a look before saying, "Well mama, Mrs. Evans, this dinner looks really good. Thanks for the meal."

He looked down at his mama's fried chicken and collared greens and Mrs. Evans biscuits and Candied yams.

"Well, I'm just so glad to have my baby back home."

"Henry, say grace," Mrs. Carrington nudged him.

Henry sighed before reciting, "God is good, God is great. Let us thank him for our food. Amen." He began to scoop some of the candied yams in his plate before passing along the food.

"So, Mama told me you were teaching two kids?" Henry asked, looking at Hannah.

"Yes, Alexandre and Nicole." Her French accent sounded smooth as she said it, as if she could just roll those words around in her mouth.

"Did they fire you or did you choose to leave? I heard Europe is getting pretty hostile towards Negros."

"They moved to Switzerland."

"Oh wow. That must've been hard," he said, his mouth in a grimace.

She evaded his eyes. "Yes, Henry it was hard because I'll miss them. But, I'm also happy to be home. I've missed Mama."

"And now you're home and we can spend a lot of time together," Mrs. Evans said.

Hannah smiled at her mom and put some potatoes in her mouth. Henry cleared his throat. "So who's been keeping you company in France? Surely you must've had some friends."

He could see Hannah fighting to control herself. "I did. Her name was Claire. She was my employer." Hannah was speaking so proper, almost sounding like a real European. She sounded different, almost ingenious.

"A white woman was your friend?" He said, looking at her with disbelief.

"She was. She taught me a great deal. Life in Paris was hard to adjust to at first and even though I could speak French, my accent needed some work. She helped me, as well as, the kids helped me settle in."

Henry chuckled. "I suppose now you'll tell me she's responsible for your makeover?"

Hannah pursed her lips and met his eyes intensely. "As a matter of fact, she is. She was the one who taught me to appreciate the way I looked. She once loved a colored soldier she met during the Great War and had no prejudices against us. She took me shopping and taught me to wear makeup. Now is there anything else you'd like to know?"

"Can this amazing woman hire me?"

"She's dead Henry. She passed a year ago. Surely your mother must've told you that. I wrote it in a letter."

He had forgotten. He heard that a friend of hers had passed, but he wasn't expecting it to be her employer. He did feel a bit bad as he saw the way her eyes got glassy before leaving his and focusing on eating.

"My condolences," he said. "Truly."

She didn't look at him and instead went back to eating before asking, "How's everything at the church?"

"Everything is good. We can't wait to have you back this Sunday," Mrs. Carrington said.

"Henry, will you be there?" Hannah said, giving him a fake smile.

"I keep telling Henry about his ways. He turned his back on the Lord," Mrs. Carrington said.

Henry could feel his patience wearing. "Church ain't my thing."

"It doesn't have to be your thing Henry. You can still go," Hannah said.

He didn't speak after, but he knew she could see his jaw tensing.

"So, how long will you be staying home, Hannah?" Mrs. Carrington said.

"For as long as I can. I'll be here until I find another governess position."

"I pray she can find a position here," her mama said, smiling.

Hannah smiled back at her mama before Mrs. Carrington spoke again, "It's so good seeing you and Henry in the same room again. You two haven't even seen each other since you finished school."

Henry continued to eat what was on his plate.

"It's a shame you two didn't spend more time with each other," her mama said.

Hannah shoved the beans around in her plate before answering, "We were very focused on our studies. We only saw each other every now and then."

Henry spoke up now, looking at the two mothers before focusing his eyes on Hannah. "We just ran in different circles. Hannah studied a whole lot and I tried to balance my studies with friends."

Hannah bit her bottom lip before responding. "Henry, you studied a lot too, in fact I saw you around Howard studying a good deal. What exactly were you studying for?"

"Architecture."

"If I didn't know any better, I thought you were studying to be a doctor, with all that anatomy."

Henry smiled now slyly. "I made sure to keep myself well rounded."

Hannah pushed one of the string beans in her mouth and chewed vigorously.

"Since you two haven't seen each other in a while, Mae and I are going to go sit on the porch for a while and let you two catch up," Henry's mama said, rising up from her seat.

"Mama, you don't have to do that," Henry said.

"Sure, we do, we know you both have things to say that you may not want your mamas to hear. Come on, Mae," she said, as she and Hannah's mama went through the door.

Hannah tapped her fingers on the table. "You haven't changed one bit, have you Henry?"

"Nope," he said, putting some potatoes in his mouth. "But you have, haven't you?"

"What's that supposed to mean?"

"I didn't say anything that's hard to understand."

"You're so full of yourself."

"And you pretend that you're not."

"Excuse me?"

He glared at her. "Oh, don't play stupid like you didn't enjoy the stunt you pulled today. You enjoyed every minute of it. You liked when I flirted with you," he chuckled. "You think because you look different now, that you'll have something over me?"

"Different? You mean that I'm not ugly anymore."

"You said it, I didn't."

"I hate you." The word hissed out of her mouth and her fingers tightened around her drinking glass.

"Ooo, and those are the words of a Christian woman."

Hannah threw the water in his face. "Now I just offered you your first baptism." She went up the stairs.

Henry wiped his face with a napkin and got up from the table, exiting the house. He heard gasps before Mrs. Evans said, "Henry, what happened to you?"

"It's nothing, I just had an accident." He examined his shirt that was clinging to his chest. "Hannah decided to go to bed early. We'll catch up another time," he said, before putting on his hat and walking out to his car.

He drove out back to Pete's. The music was booming and he could hear the laughter of women being twirled on the dance floor from outside. The entertainers were mostly at the Paradise and Flamingo Club, but, Pete would get a few good singers after they'd finished performing there, or if both places had been booked out. Pete would get amateur acts, who'd sometimes get good reviews and then be promoted to the Paradise or Flamingo Club. Maureen would probably be here tonight. He could spend some time with her after he was done dancing and getting a few drinks.

Pete's was mostly filled with people under thirty years old. It wasn't as fancy as the other clubs that were fashioned after the country clubs like the Paradise Club. Instead it was always filled with young people ready to drink, listen to the most outrageous songs, and dance the dirtiest moves they'd heard about. Not to mention the exotic dancers that would come through there, even "Lottie the Body" had once paid a visit. Henry was met with greetings and went straight to the bar, getting a beer and sitting down on the stool next to Pete.

"I thought you weren't coming tonight."

"Yeah, well my plans changed," Henry said, turning the bottle up to his mouth.

"Why you wet?"

Henry laughed. "She threw water on me."

"Who?"

"Hannah."

"Sweet Hannah? Why? You must've really ticked her off."

"Nah, I only just messed with her head," Henry said, drinking some more and turning to Pete. "She's different. She ain't the Hannah we remember." Pete offered him a cigarette and he shook his head no.

"What you mean she's not the same?"

"She's different....Pete she looks sweet. *Real* sweet."

Pete chuckled. "Well, I'll be. France did her some good. Told you, Henry, she probably been with some white man. Changed her."

"Hannah ain't been with no white man."

"Whatever you say."

Henry finished his beer and set in back on the bar, tapping his feet to the sounds of *In the Mood*.

He saw Maureen coming towards him, her black dress, cut in a V, showing an ample amount of her breasts. Her bright red lipstick contrasted against her light cream-colored skin.

"Hey," she said, before kissing him full on the mouth. "I've missed you."

"I can see that."

Maureen smiled seductively. "You gonna spend the whole night sitting or are you gonna dance?"

"I can twirl you around for a bit."

Henry joined her on the dance floor. He buried his face in her neck as they swayed.

"What are you doing tonight?" He whispered in her ear.

"Hopefully, spending it with you."

"mhmm..." he said nibbling on her ear.

"Do you want to leave now?"

"Don't be too eager."

She looked embarrassed. He raised her chin. "Later. Ok? Let's just enjoy the moment now."

She nodded and looked away. He'd been with Maureen for years and it made sense to get married, but he didn't want to get married. Maureen was nice, she was pretty, she just wasn't all that special to be honest. They could have a great time together, it made him sound like a pig, but she was great in bed and that was it. He couldn't talk to her about life. He couldn't come to her after a day of getting turned down by another man saying they didn't need anymore Negro workers. So, he just drank and then fooled around with her for a bit. He knew that she was hoping that one day he'd wake up and change his mind about her. That wasn't going to happen and he was honest with her on that. But, she stuck around, so he reasoned that she knew what she was getting herself into.

After another half hour of dancing and another glass of whiskey, he went back to her place. He couldn't tell you what he thought of when he was making love to Maureen, he thought of lots of things, everything except her.

Afterwards, she got up, putting on a robe. "Are you hungry?"

"Nah, I think I'm gonna go," he said, rising up and putting on his clothes.

Her eyes looked embarrassed. "Ok. I'll see you around."

"Alright, goodnight," he said, as he headed out the door.

Henry looked up and saw that the moon was full against the velvet navy sky. The night was still alive with the hoots and hollers of the rich colored folks who'd high tail it out of here before the harsh winter came. He could see their figures by the lake, still skating on the rink they set up there in the summer. His mother told him that when his pa died that she'd seen something in the paper about a Black Eden where the land was reasonable and colored folks were treated fair. She said she had nothing left to lose and decided to take all her money and get out of Mississippi. Henry put his hat on and headed to his car. He had worked like crazy to afford it. Not many residents in Idlewild had a car, especially with the Depression and all. It was a miracle Henry could afford it himself. The good thing for him was that he never put any money in banks. He had saved away enough so that he could maybe start his own business someday. But he still needed the extra funding to get all the permits and hire workers. But, those dreams seemed farther and farther away.

He drove home, feeling the cool night air on him. A sudden memory came back to him of when he was thirteen and he nearly broke his arm climbing up to see Hannah one night. Hannah's room became his haven whenever he had nightmares where he was stuck back in the south. There deep in the woods he'd find dangling bodies, their bulging eyes, once he'd even seen a body floating in the river, a boulder tied around the neck. He would always go to Hannah's room when those memories returned, and spend the rest of the night sleeping on her floor until early morning. Then he'd retreat back to his room before anyone could see. He had built a ladder but that night the ladder fell backwards, knocking the wind out of him and having him clutching his arm for days. Hannah had helped him up and slept in his room that night, just to make sure he was ok. She had felt warm as she curled against him. Once, someone from school had asked if he'd ever slept with Hannah and he could've said yes. But he said no, knowing what they'd meant and not wanting to ruin Hannah's reputation.

He looked up to the window of her room and he wondered if she really meant that she hated him. He could see the curtain over her window, billowing in the breeze. He wished for a moment that he could take that ladder and climb into her room and tell her how horrible it was to be stuck in a world where you couldn't move ahead, no matter how hard you tried. But that was a long time ago. College, Paris, the Depression, and the war had changed them. So he just pushed the door open to his house, careful not to wake his mama and dozed off to sleep.

Henry woke with the familiar throbbing pain in his head. He opened his eyes and looked at the blue walls. His room was the only one in the house that wasn't white. He'd painted it himself when he was fourteen. Blue. It was the color that calmed him the most. It was the color of the sky, the lakes, the color of the work shirt his dad used to wear, that he still kept to this day. It was the only thing he'd kept from his pa. He used to try it on every few months when he was younger to see if he was growing, getting bigger, becoming the man his pa was. Now it just stayed in the top drawer of his dresser.

He heard talking in the kitchen. He looked in the mirror and ran a hand through his curly, dark brown hair. His mama and pa were both mulattoes and they'd passed on their hair as well as their caramel colored skin. He had his mother's green colored eyes that had gotten him taunts from the kids back in the South. "Puss eyes" they'd call him and those eyes had been swollen many times with a purple ring around them until he learned how to fight. Growing into his Pa's six-foot plus, 220-pound frame had also helped matters later when he moved here. Rubbing his eyes, he went to the shower to freshen up, and then headed downstairs to see his mother and Mrs. Evans talking.

"Henry! I was about to come up there and drag you out that bed."

"Morning, Mama. Morning, Mrs. Evans" he said, kissing their cheeks and then heading to the stove to pour himself some coffee.

"Morning," they both said. Both of the mothers had maintained slim figures, probably due to them always insisting on walking everywhere. His mama though was fiery in a way that Hannah's mama wasn't. They balanced each other out. Fire and water, he would call them sometimes. His mama could send someone packing if they crossed her, while Mae Evans was more conservative in values and character.

"We were waiting for you," his mom said.

"Am I in trouble?" he said, giving them a smile.

"No, Mrs. Evans wants to know if you could take Hannah into town to buy a few things and I told her you wouldn't mind."

"Now, why would you tell Mrs. Evans something like that?" he said, sitting at the table.

"Henry," his mom said, eying him.

He looked back at his mom before turning to Mrs. Evans. "Tell her I'll be there in an hour."

"Good," Mrs. Evans said, as she smiled and got up from the table. "Now I have to find her. She went on the other side of the lake because the beach side is *too noisy* with tourists. "

"She still does that?"

"Yes, I had to shoo her out the house. She wanted to cook breakfast and clean on her first day back."

Henry chuckled and thought about the times they'd gone to the lake as kids, daring each other to jump in even when the water was frigid. His mama nearly took the switch to him when Hannah had gotten pneumonia when they were 11. He noticed that she'd started going there after school. Probably to avoid the teasing she used to get, since he'd stop coming to her rescue. Plus, she hadn't talked to him after the incident with Maureen. Mrs. Evans left and Henry remained at the table with his mom.

"Henry, promise me you'll be nice."

"Mama, I am nice. She's the one that threw the water."

"I bet you deserved it."

He chuckled. "And all the women gang up on the man."

"You already know that I've always had Hannah as the next Mrs. Carrington."

Henry shook his head. "Ma, I love you, but I already told you, there won't be another Mrs. Carrington."

"I'm your mama, I know better. You see how pretty she is? Smart, caring...Henry she's the best girl around here."

Henry scraped his finger against the old table. "You and Mrs. Evans are plotting and it's not gonna work. I'm not looking for a wife."

"You're just looking for someone to lay with."

Henry nearly spit his coffee.

"Didn't think I knew about that? The Black Casanova. You're not quite as slick as you think."

Henry looked down at his coffee cup, not wanting to meet her eyes.

"Listen, just promise me Hannah won't be some conquest for you. If you don't plan on something serious, then hands off."

He held up his hands in surrender. "I promise."

"Good. Now, I'm going to tend to the roses and then I'm going to do a bit of fishing."

"Ok, Mama, I'll see you later then."

"Have fun with Hannah. Not too much though," she said, smiling before she left.

Henry shook his head. Yes, Hannah had come back pretty as a picture. He could still remember her in that pink dress with her matching hat. He would love to take her for a night, but he wouldn't let her get under his skin. Hannah was too stuffy and boring, nothing like the women he was with now. Plus, he liked his women more experienced, not virgins who would fumble around in the dark. Hannah probably didn't even know how to kiss. He was certain he was still the only man she'd ever kissed. He took out his drawing book and sketched a few more drawings to add to his portfolio. Turned over the pages, the sketches of houses and buildings flickered by as he turned. Houses and buildings that he'd never get to build. He turned over the page and started the outline Hannah's face as she sat waiting on that train bench. He drew her body before finishing the details on the dress and her hat that framed her heart shaped face. It was an exact replica of her. Why had he drawn Hannah? He moved to throw it out, but instead tucked it into his portfolio because it really was a good sketch. He opened the door to leave to go to the Evans house when he saw Hannah at the porch. He took her in for a few moments. She was wearing a light yellow dress with her dark brown hair pulled away from her face and just the slightest hint of red lipstick on her full lips.

"I was heading over to your house. You didn't have to walk," Henry said, looking into her almond shaped brown eyes.

"It's hardly what I consider a walk."

"Well, since you enjoy walking so much, why didn't you walk into town?"

She rolled her eyes. "Mama insisted you take me."

He walked over to her and turned her around, looking her up and down.

"I beg your pardon!" There she was again with that British sound. She'd probably had to talk like that so much overseas that it had stuck to her like sticky glue.

"Sorry, just checking if you have any weapons on you." It was true, but it gave him a chance to survey her shapely body as well.

She looked angry enough to sock him. "Would you like to check my purse as well, Henry?"

"As a matter of fact I would."

She tucked her purse underneath her arm. "If I had a weapon, trust me, I would've used it already."

He smiled. "I thought ladies were supposed to be meek."

"Meek. Not stupid."

They stood there a few moments before Henry said, "We should go now."

They got into the car and neither spoke for a while. "Where'd you get the money to buy this car?" Hannah asked.

"Bootlegging."

Her eyes widened. "Henry!"

He nearly bust his gut laughing. "I'm joking. I work Hannah." He started driving along the dirt roads.

"Where?"

The day was nice, not too hot or cool, just right, with barely any clouds. "Construction. Building some new stuff out by Baldwin and Reed City."

"Wow. So you made it? Achieved your goal, despite your womanizing, heathen ways," she said, smirking.

The barb hurt more than she'd intended. "No, I don't have my own business. Still working for some white developers. But for the summer it's easy finding work around here building some more hotels and doghouses."

"Oh..." she said, looking sheepish. "I'm sorry. I didn't intend on being so mean."

"I'm a big boy, Hannah. I can take it."

He looked over at her and she looked away quickly. "Still, I shouldn't have. Men are often sensitive about their work. It's an extension of their manhood."

He laughed. "Says the woman who's never actually been with a man."

"You act like it's a bad thing."

He glanced back at her and smiled. "No, it's not a bad thing for a girl like you."

She folded her arms. "A girl like me?"

"Yes, the pure, church type. Your innocence will find you a husband."

"And I bet when you're done sowing your wild oats you'll want a 'pure, church girl'?"

"Nope."

"What kind of woman would you want?"

"One who satisfies me in every way."

She blushed, looking flustered. "You're disgusting."

"I thought you were old enough to talk about things like this now."

She continued to look out the window and folded her arms over her chest. "I don't want to talk about this anymore."

Henry laughed and resumed driving. When they reached town, Hannah looked out the car, taking in the new fresh log houses that served as stores. The big wooden structures that served as country clubs, dance clubs, and restaurants for the rich, complete with the bustle of the cars. Idlewild was really "The Black Eden" as they called it. It was beautiful just about every time of year, except winter. Winters here in Michigan were harsh, the lake effect pummeling them with snow, trapping everyone inside their homes.

"It looks different now, doesn't it?"

"Yes," she said softly, taking in the new stores.

He parked the car and went to her side to open the door, but she'd already helped herself. "I'm not your girl, so you don't have to be chivalrous. I can vote, so I can open the door for myself too." He shook his head; he wished his Mama had been here to witness why he could never marry Hannah. She knew how to get under his skin.

"So where do you plan to go? To the bookstore?" he said, mocking her.

"Yes, as a matter of fact I am. I also need to get some clothes as well."

"Well, I don't intend on following you all day long so I'll be at Pete's."

"Pete's?"

"The club. It's not too far. Just come by when you're done."

She stammered. "I..I.."

"Don't want to be seen at a club?"

"That's not it."

"I bet it is. In fact, I bet you've never been to one."

Her eyes flashed something fierce. But before she could respond he said, "Look, I will meet you back here in two hours." He walked away before she could say anything. She would mostly likely just spend the next couple hours staying in the bookstore gathering as much as she could. When they were little, she used to go to Mr. Cooper's bookstore and spend hours in there. Sometimes he'd just give her the books for free because he liked her so much, and knew that their mamas didn't have a whole lot of money to spend on those things. When he got to Pete's he sat down exhausted on the seat.

"You here during the day again?"

Henry shook his head. "Had to take Hannah shopping."

Pete laughed, his voice cackling. He took out a cigarette and held out one for Henry. Henry held up his hand to say no. "She definitely your woman now."

Henry smiled. "Just get me some whiskey old man."

Pete poured him a glass and set it down in front of him. "So let me guess? You've already poured on your charm."

Henry swallowed some of the drink feeling it warm him. "She says I'm not charming."

"You're gonna prove her wrong though."

"Of course."

He went back to his task of cleaning the glasses while Henry took another drink. "I take it you don't approve?"

"I don't."

"Why not? Never had a problem with me chasing skirts before."

"Hannah ain't like them other girls."

"Pete, I know that."

"I ain't your pa and I don't tell no grown man how to live his life. But just consider the girl and don't mess with her."

Henry sighed. "Ok, you have my word. I won't mess with Hannah."

"Good," he said, giving a slight smile. "That is, unless you fall for her."

"You're *real* funny."

"You don't think a girl like that would make you fall in love?"

Henry set down his drink. "The one I left at the bookstore? Hell no."

"Why not?"

"Did you not see my wet shirt last night? She's the most stubborn woman I've met. She knows *exactly* how to tick me off."

"I'd say ya'll are match made in heaven. You need someone to challenge your black behind."

"Nah, she'll give me grey hairs like yours in no time."

Pete laughed. "Listen boy, I've been hearing that Dr. Dan left behind some money to help build a fancy new hotel and a friend of his decided to pick up the task of getting workers."

Dr. Daniel Hale Williams was the first surgeon of color to successfully do open heart surgery and he, W.E.B Dubois, and

Madame CJ Walker owned a good deal of land up here before their deaths.

"They say who's heading it?" Henry asked.

"They're looking for an architect."

Henry leaned back a bit on the stool. "Who's his friend?"

"Dr. Kingston. Don't know him, but are you gonna look into it?"

"Yes, but I'm gonna have to fish around to get more information. If you run into someone, get as much information as you can. Say it's for a friend. Offer them another drink if you have to."

"Are you gonna pay for that extra drink?"

Henry smiled and put down two dollars on the counter. "Will that cover it?"

"Sure will."

He sat around and talked for a while, telling Pete he needed to buff the floors again, and helping Pete with his ledgers. When all the numbers were done being recorded, Henry got up. "Gotta go pick up Princess Hannah." He heard Pete's laughter as he exited and walked back towards the car.

He saw her come out of a store, her yellow dress blowing in the slight breeze as she tried to haul all her boxes towards the car. She looked up and saw him.

"Does the voting woman need help?"

Hannah gritted her teeth. "Just help me."

He smirked before grabbing up some of the boxes and carrying them to the car. She carried some too and tried to lay them inside the car carefully before one got away from her and toppled to the floor of the car, spilling its contents. Henry looked down and saw lace, cotton and silk undergarments littered against the car floor. Her eyes grew wide as she hurried to stuff them back inside the box.

"Nothing to be ashamed of. I've seen it all." He hadn't seen *her* in those lacy under things and he sure wanted to. He was sure they'd look perfect as they curved around her breasts and hips.

Hannah didn't say anything and just hurried into the car. Henry joined her but she wouldn't look him in the eye. He chuckled.

"You're really making this worse than it is."

"How would you feel if I'd seen your-"

He grinned. "Oh trust me I wouldn't be embarrassed. I might enjoy it actually."

She hit him in the arm. "Beast!"

He laughed uncontrollably now. He wasn't sure if it was her newfound accent or her embarrassment that made him laugh more.

She looked at him quizzically before leaning over and smelling him. "Henry Carrington? Have you been drinking?"

He looked at her, amusement still in his eyes. "Yes, mother. I had a few drinks. Are you going to tear my hide?"

"This is not funny. I do not want a drunk man driving me." She moved to open the door. "Let me drive!"

"First of all, I'm not drunk. Second, I won't have a woman driving me around. Third, do you even know how to drive?"

"Yes, I know how to drive and if you had one ounce of pride you wouldn't drive a lady after drinking."

"You're *not* driving."

"I am too, or I will stay here and you will have to explain why I walked, or had to receive a ride from another man."

"Fine by me."

Hannah huffed before leaving the car. "You're not a gentleman, Henry!"

"Never claimed to be. I will leave your things on your porch."

"Fine!" Hannah said, turning away from him. He waited for a few moments, waiting to see if her stubbornness would break. "Suit yourself," he said, before driving off.

Damn woman! Ok, maybe he didn't help matters but she was just so combative. He couldn't just leave her out to get a ride from anyone so he drove along the backside of town, so she couldn't see his car. He parked and figured he'd wait around fifteen minutes and let her cool off before going back for her. He went back around and saw her talking to Jeffrey Olsen in a crisp tan suit, with his matching blue handkerchief, tie, and shirt. He was the biggest ass he'd ever met. He was a smooth talking lawyer who had cheated dozens of people out of money, including Henry. Then to make things worse he had most people blackmailed so they were too afraid to press charges. He was just about to go get her when he saw Olsen gather her things in his car and she hopped in next to him and they drove off.

He gripped the steering wheel tight. Putting the car in drive, he sped out of town, the trees scraping against the sides of the car, as he turned trying to take shortcuts to beat them home. He hoped they wouldn't leave scratches on his car. When he got home, thankfully they weren't there, but of course Mama and Mrs. Evans railed at him for leaving her. Mama got even madder because he'd been drinking. They all sat out on the Evan's porch waiting for her, and he didn't think he could possibly be more ticked off until he saw her drive up with Jeffrey Olsen, laughing and smiling.

"Oh Hannah, thank God you're home," Mr. Evans said.

Both he and Olsen sized one another up, not saying a word.

"Yes, Jeffrey was nice enough to give me a ride home."

Jeffrey spoke up, "Yes, I couldn't very well leave her stranded," he said, looking at Henry, whose jaw tightened.

"Thank you, Mr. Olsen," Mrs. Evans said.

"Thank you, Jeffrey," Hannah said, smiling shyly.

"My pleasure, Hannah," he said. "Well, I should be heading on back. Hopefully I'll see you again."

Hannah smiled shyly as he left and drove off.

"You took a ride from Olsen?" Henry asked.

"I'm sorry I wasn't left with many options," Hannah said, anger making her nostrils flare. "Besides he was nice. Smart too, and he speaks some French."

"I was coming back for you."

"Well, it seems that Jeffrey beat you to it."

"I don't think you should be around him. He's a con artist."

"Yeah right, he couldn't be worse than you!"

"Enough!" Mrs. Carrington yelled coming in between them. "Now, Henry I told you to take her and bring her back."

"She wouldn't drive back with me!"

"You were drunk!"

"I told you I wasn't drunk," Henry gritted out.

"Stop it, you two!" Mrs. Carrington said. "Hannah stay away from Olsen and Henry you owe Hannah for that stunt you pulled."

"What?!"

"You heard me."

"Mama, I'm a grown man. I don't owe her a thing."

"Grown men don't drive around a lady smelling like whiskey."

Henry's jaw tightened. "I'm sorry Hannah. Next time perhaps you shouldn't be so stubborn."

"Next time you should let me drive."

"You really wanna drive?"

"Sure do."

He tossed her the keys. "Take the car for a few days. That's my payment to you." He started to walk back to his house before yelling out, "And don't you dare wreck it!"

He'd been watching her movements with his car. Sunday, she'd only taken it to carry their mothers to church. Henry stayed in bed sleeping and then worked on some sketches of the courthouse he'd heard about.

Monday, she'd taken the car out for a drive, and when Henry came outside to walk to work, he looked straight at her before yelling, "Don't wreck my car, woman!" Her response had been to stick her tongue out at him.

"Is that the best you can do?" He yelled back.

Then she revved the engine, peeling the tires, circled the car around him and sped off, causing dirt to hail on him. He choked on dust and the rest of the men walking to work laughed and hooted. Even Hannah had looked shocked at her own actions. *Good*, he flustered her as much as she flustered him. Each night at dinner when he asked, she'd only reported that she'd driven out to the lake and spent the day reading, watched the workers build houses across the lake, and napped under the sun. As expected, each night he teased her that she was wasting away her week with his car.

"You call driving to the lake a joy ride? I thought you were more interesting than that?"

Hannah replied with a dig. "Would you like me to drive into town and visit Jeffrey? Perhaps that would be interesting."

He looked up at her with cold eyes. "Go right ahead if you're looking for trouble."

"Trouble?"

"Yes, Missy."

It was Friday now and he would probably take back the car from her tonight after he came home from Pete's. Fridays and Saturdays were usually the liveliest nights at the club and now they had some famous people coming in every other night. Everyone always waited in anticipation of who it would be. He headed in feeling free especially because he knew his mama and Mrs. Evans were away and he wouldn't have to worry about waking her. When he got there, everyone gave their greetings. He saw a beauty out on the dance floor in a deep purple dress that had a bit of shimmer to it, it showed off her tiny waist and wide hips. She smiled his way and he walked over and asked her to dance. Her name was Ruby and she spent the rest of the night hanging on to him like a leech. I mean she wasn't gonna be good for much more than a roll in the hay because she couldn't even engage him in simple conversation. Only kept redirecting any small talk to see where he lived and how much money he had in his wallet. He heard his friend Robert from work yell out his name.

Henry looked over to see Robert bringing over some tall light skinned man. He looked at his brown pants, striped shirt, red suspenders, and expensive cufflinks and shoes.

"This man says he could beat you to a drinking contest!" Robert said, incredulously. "I told him he's crazy."

"Well, that's too bad, Mr.-"

"Parker."

"Mr. Parker, " Henry said. "I'm not going home wasted tonight."

"Would you be willing to go home $50 richer?"

Henry smiled. "You'd bet so high?"

"I would," he said, adjusting his suspenders.

Henry knew his type. Too much money and no idea what to do with it. "You're on. Fifty it is."

They sat at the bar and Robert told Pete the bet and Pete set a shot of gin in front of both of them. They did drink after drink as the room became more hazy and the crowd grew loud with intensity. He was swimming after the eighth shot, but he kept going, not willing to let this rich boy out do him. He saw a flash of emerald green emerge from the crowd and he thought he saw Hannah's face swimming in front of him, before the face disappeared again. He shook it off as illusion. Parker started to vomit, the crowd cheered, Robert held up his hand like he'd won a boxing match, and slapped the fifty in his hand. Ruby kissed him and he still felt like he was swirling.

"Let's get out of here," Ruby said.

She led him out and he felt her touch him and soon he was kissing her against the side of the building. He could feel her hands roaming and his started roaming too over the planes of her body.

Suddenly he felt someone snatch Ruby away.

"What the hell are you doing with him?!" a man yelled at her. Henry felt his anger rise and swung, hitting him. The man staggered and spit before coming back to punch Henry in his stomach, making him feel breathless. If he wasn't so drunk, he'd be able to at least focus and fight back.

"Who do you think you are, messing with my girl?!" Henry saw a group of men surround him now and he felt the first blow that sent him to the ground. He couldn't tell which direction the rest of blows were coming from except that the pain was intense. He'd said before that the worst pain he'd experienced was the gripping stomach pains he'd gotten at Howard after he accepted a twenty dollar bet to eat week-old shellfish. He'd nearly died from the pain and vomiting. It was the only time he'd ever been in the hospital. Every time he'd made a bet, something went wrong. Like now. Each time he took a breath he'd feel another kick in the stomach, back, or a punch to his ribs.

"Stop! Please!" He thought it might be Ruby, but he couldn't mistake her voice. Hannah.

The men eased away from him and he moaned on the ground, rolling over in pain.

Ruby's boyfriend got close to her and Henry could see Hannah's stillness in her green dress. "Is he your man?"

"No," she said. Henry wanted to speak, but taking a breath hurt like hell.

"So why you defending him? He deserves this."

"He's my friend. Please. I think you've done enough to him."

Ruby's boyfriend examined her and he could see Hannah shaking.

"I should take you instead. To teach him a lesson about taking someone's girl." Henry now tried to get up, but failed. He couldn't let this guy take advantage of Hannah.

"I told you I'm not his girl."

He laughed. "Nah, I think I want you."

Henry moaned and tried to get up when he heard the sound of a gun clicking.

"Leave her alone," he heard a man's voice say and he laid down against the ground, trying to fight against the pain in his stomach and his ribs.

"Alright," Ruby's boyfriend said. "We're leaving."

Hannah moved closer to Henry, but the man reached down once more and punched Henry so hard that he knocked out cold.

Henry woke to the sounds of the car he was in and felt the night air. Next came the painful reminder of what had taken place. His whole body was throbbing in pain.

"Shh it's ok. It's Hannah. We're going home," she said, gently touching him.

He eased back against the seat, remaining quiet and groaning whenever the car jerked him around on the dirt road. He smelt the slight fragrance of smoke on her.

"You smell like smoke."

He could see the embarrassment on her face even in the night. "I was smoking a cigarette before I saw you and the guys."

A cigarette? Hannah smoked? He nearly choked on his laughter as pain shot through his stomach and ribs.

"Are you alright?" she asked him.

"No, your cigarette smoking is killing me," he said, teasing her. But, she turned away from him, not sensing the humor in his comment.

When she pulled up to her house she stopped the car and hurried to his side to help him. The sound of critters filled the air.

"I can manage," he said, trying to ease himself out the car but staggering.

"Let me help," she said, ignoring him and carrying some of his weight as they both staggered to the door. "Henry, you weigh a ton. Mrs. Carrington has been feeding you too much," she said, trying to lighten the mood. He looked at her, his right eye's vision limited and he knew that it would be completely swollen shut by morning. "Jeffrey helped me get you in the car."

Henry felt his anger quicken. "You should've let me walk on my own."

"As if you could."

Hannah opened the front door and Henry staggered inside.

"Sit at the kitchen table. I'm going to get something cold for your eye."

He sat down exhausted and Hannah handed him some ice and he held it to his eye while she went to the stove heating a kettle and moving to gather some rags and a basin. Her house was much different than his. Mrs. Evans actually cared about the decor in her house. Everything always seemed in order and matched. The kitchen was light yellow, the same light yellow he'd painted in Hannah's room almost ten years ago. There were the green curtains that Mrs. Evans had sewn and put up. It was Henry's mama who'd really gotten Mrs. Evans into sewing, in turn for teaching her how to make her candied yams. While Mrs. Evans' mamas yams were good, but they were never as good as his mama's. But Mrs. Evans had sure beaten his mom at the sewing thing.

When the water heated, Hannah poured it into the basin and went to his side. "This will hurt a bit." She put the hot towel to his face and he winced, pulling back. "I have to do this." She put the rag to his face again and started to clean the blood and the cuts on his face. "You shouldn't have been messing with that man's girl."

He moved the ice from his eye and looked at her with annoyance. He didn't even want to talk about Olsen helping him out or what the hell she was doing with him at Pete's.

"Sorry. I know you value honesty. Perhaps I'm being too honest, too soon," Hannah said, moving to the kitchen sink to clean the rag. "If it's worth anything, I think he's a coward for not fighting you fair. I know you would've whooped him." She moved back to him and sat down as he looked at her intensely.

"I thought you hated me," he said.

She gave a faint smile and he noticed the way the dim lighting was playing against her skin. "Not today. You're hurt."

He tried to smile, but his lip was busted. She continued to tend to his face. "At least you didn't lose any teeth. I think that would've put a huge damper on your love life." He couldn't help but smile at that.

"Thank you," he said, holding her gaze with his good eye. "I won't embarrass you by making you tend to my chest. I'll do it myself."

She didn't insist and he knew that she was probably truly embarrassed. "You can stay the night in Mama's room."

"Aren't you worried about the gossip when I leave here in the morning?"

"There would be gossip anyway. I'm sure someone saw me drive home with you and let you in."

"Are you getting brave?"

"I stood up to those guys, what do you think?"

"Touché."

He rose to go up the stairs, the pain racking his body. By the time he made it up to Mrs. Evans' room, he was winded. He was ready to take off his shirt and tend to himself when he saw a light approach him.

"Henry." She was fumbling her with hands.

"Yes," he said, turning to her.

"I know we're too old for this and I don't want you to think I'm being forward. Can I stay in here? With you?" She looked innocent in her light blue nightgown; the lamplight accentuating her eyes and the shine of the silk scarf tied around her hair.

He sat back down. "Why? Are you scared?"

She looked down, embarrassed. "A little."

"He won't come back here. He doesn't know where you live Hannah."

"It's not that," she whispered.

He looked at her in the dim light. "Then what is it?"

"I didn't tell you this before. Do you know why my mama moved us from Texas?

"Yeah, your Daddy got killed in the war."

"Yes, and she was afraid she'd lose me too."

He sat down on the bed and she sat next to him. "My best friend Nance and I were walking home from school and we saw some white men drinking and laughing. They had a colored man with them and they were beating him. We were about to leave when they saw us. They dragged us out of the woods and made us stand there as they made the noose for him. They reeked of liquor. Kept laughing in our faces. Told us we would watch him hang and know what would happen to uppity niggers." Hannah fumbled with her hands. "Nance was shaking so bad and we held hands and started crying. The colored man managed to grab one of their guns and shoot one of them. He told us to run. And we did. We ran like hell. That night, Nance's house got burned down. Mama and I had to hide with some friends. She took all the money Pa had saved and bought us some train tickets."

Henry looked at her intensely. "Why didn't you tell me this before?"

"I don't like talking about it and I didn't want it to trigger nightmares for you about the South again."

He nodded and noticed her curls pinned under her scarf. "That's why you hate liquor."

"The smell reminds me of the men."

"Well, then I won't subject you to it tonight. Sleep on the bed. I'll take the floor."

"Henry, you're busted up. You can't sleep on the floor."

"Hannah," he said, exasperated. "For once, please don't argue. Take the bed."

She looked at him before laying down across the bed, the sounds of rustling sheets filling his ears.

He looked in her direction. "Please don't poke fun now," she said.

"I'm not. I was just wondering if you were scared while you were in Paris."

She smiled grimly. "Yes. The family I worked for, they're Jews. There was a lot of terror and they had to get to somewhere safe."

"You too, I suppose."

"Yes," she said as she looked up at the ceiling. "I would look at all these white people and to be honest, if it wasn't for that damned star they make them wear, I'd have no clue who was a Jew and who wasn't."

"But you'd never be able to hide."

She looked at him and pointed to her dark hand. "No kidding." She looked away again. "I don't know what I'd do if something happened to those children. I'm only grateful that Claire passed and didn't have to see them flee France in terror."

He sat on the edge of the bed. "I'm glad you're safe."

She smiled faintly. "I'm glad they didn't do you any worse. I really got scared when I saw them beating you."

He cleared his throat. "Goodnight Hannah."

"Goodnight Henry."

He went to tend to himself and by the time he came back she was asleep. He turned off the lamp and went to bed.

Henry woke a little before dawn and gathered his shirt that was spotted with blood. Hannah was asleep on the bed, curled up, the sheet wrapped around her, sleeping peacefully. He owed her, and he'd start by getting out of here before any more gossip could build. Discreetly of course. His body ached from lying on the wood floor all night. He eased out, remembering the old way he used to exit the house, without anyone noticing. His body was filled with purple splotches and he groaned as he moved about. At least he had the weekend to heal up before he went to work on Monday, although he was certain he'd still be bruised and the guys would all tease him for days. His head was also raging from all that gin.

Opening the door to his house, he went straight to the shower, washing off the dirt and sweat. It hurt to have to scrub his bruised skin. He wanted to find that guy and beat the crap out of him. That girl didn't mention anything about having a man. Who knows where they could've driven all the way from? He settled in his bed to lie down, drifting off when he heard knocking. He ignored it, but the knocking grew louder, and he pulled on a pair of trousers before going downstairs to open the door.

"What!" he said, gruffly before seeing Hannah there. Her eyes were surprised, but that didn't lessen the beauty that stood before him. Her long hair was curled and framed her face; she wore no lipstick, just a simple day dress with a floral design. In fact, her face appeared just as natural as if she had just rose from bed. She was holding a covered plate in her hand.

"I just wanted to see how you were doing because you sneaked out on me."

He felt bad. "I'm sorry, I just thought I'd get out before anyone noticed I'd spent the night."

"Oh," she said, looking down shyly, and he noticed then she wouldn't meet his eyes because he wasn't wearing a shirt.

"I was sleeping. Don't usually sleep in a shirt." She met his eyes trying hard not to focus on his chest. He chuckled, "Come in. I'll put on a shirt so I don't tempt you."

She came in and he closed the door. "Listen Mr. Swelled Head, you do not tempt me."

So, now the Hannah he was used to showed up. She was even starting to drop that fake accent. Michigan was seeping back into her veins. "Oh really," he said, folding his arms across his chest. So I can remain shirtless?"

"No, goodness, you're so improper."

He laughed. "You and your pride," he said, pulling a shirt on and sitting down at the table while he buttoned up himself. "So what do you have there?"

"I brought you breakfast."

He cocked his head to the side and looked at her for a while. "Surely you're not spoiling me?"

"You're injured. Look at your face."

"Yes, but in your words and the words of that baboon, I deserved this. I should make my own damn breakfast," he said, rolling up his sleeves.

She looked down. "You didn't deserve such a brutal beating. It should've only been man to man."

"Well, the next time it will be. And I won't be generous with him."

She met his eyes. "Henry, that's a foolish idea."

"Really?" he said, sarcasm lacing his words.

"Yes. Leave things as they are before you incite a war and he decides to do more than just have his boys beat you to a pulp."

"And what makes you think so?"

She sat down across from him. "His eyes. He's not a nice man. I'm sure that girl of his probably suffered a fate close to yours."

Henry was glad he didn't hurt her. He knew he'd probably deal with guilt for an eternity had Hannah's innocence have been taken in violence. "Well, um thanks for the breakfast, but really, you don't need to do anything more for me. I'm a big boy. I can take care of myself." He looked down. "And I don't need Olsen helping out either."

"And you talk about my pride," she said, softly.

"What were you doing with him anyways? You seeing him now?"

She raised an eyebrow. "You should be a bit more grateful to him for saving both of our behinds."

He was about to speak when she continued. "And no, I went there by myself. He just happened to be there at the right time."

He smirked. "Probably stalking you."

"Well, that won't earn him a date, so that should give you peace of mind."

He couldn't help but smile. Few women he knew had her wit and sass. She cleared her throat. "Your car is parked outside. I had a good time with her."

"Her?"

"Yes," she said, blushing. "I named her."

"May I ask what?"

"That's for me to know and for you to wonder," she said, as she winked and headed out.

That girl was a spit fire. It was a shame he'd promised his mother that he wouldn't mess with her. He wondered if her kisses would be as fiery as her personality. He marveled how she could be so virginal and shy one moment and spicy the next. She had certainly grown up in more than one way. He didn't know this new Hannah and the strange thing is that he wanted to know her, wanted to know her in the way he had all those years ago. Truthfully, now that he saw her, he wanted her physically too, but it was best that he'd just offer her friendship. He opened the plate to see bacon and pancakes. He took a bite. Damn, she could cook too!

"What in God's name happened to your face?!" Was the response he heard later that night when his mother came through the door.

"Mama, I just got into a fight at Pete's. I got ambushed."

"What did you do to get a beating like this?" she said, as she turned his face to look at it.

"You don't wanna know Ma."

"I believe you," she said, shaking her head and setting her stuff down.

"Who tended to your face?"

"Hannah."

Her eyebrows rose in surprise. "You came to Hannah to fix you up?"

"No, she was at Pete's when it happened."

"Henry, I don't think Mae will like knowing that Hannah went there with all that booze. She could've been hurt."

"Ma, I didn't know she was gonna be there. Plus, Hannah is a woman. She can handle herself. She did pretty good for herself last night."

His mom sighed. "Ok," she said, as she went over and started to heat the kettle for some tea. "You need to stop all that drinking and carrying on Henry. Look what it's gotten you, a busted up face and body. Your daddy would have a fit. "

He felt the shame wash over him. He went over and kissed her cheek. "I'm fine. Really I am."

She waved him off. "Go on. You don't listen to me anyhow."

He marched out the house frustrated at himself. He never even knew his Daddy. His ma had given birth while his pa was away at war and then had gotten the letter that he had been gunned down in battle. But he always heard stories of how he looked just like him. How his Daddy was a carpenter, could lift almost anything, how he was smart to boot, and could do most math in his head faster than a person could say their address. But, that didn't stop him from being called a nigger. It didn't stop him from having to say "yes suh" and "no mam" to those bastards in the South.

He knew his mama never meant no harm bringing up that his daddy would've been disappointed. But each time it did sting.

Who wanted to know that their pa would be rolling in his grave at the disappointment their only son had become?

Lamplight flickered in the Evans house and he looked over to see that it was coming from Hannah's room. He owed her a visit, but would probably wait until he stopped looking like a creature from the underworld. Her confession last night still resonated with him. He'd always assumed that Hannah had been sheltered from the horrors of racism, since she'd never talked about it. The figures hanging from the trees were terrifying, let alone being dragged out to watch and think that you were next. Most times men were lynched, but sometimes you'd see or read in the paper about a woman or even a child. It didn't matter how old or the gender. All that qualified for being lynched was forgetting to say ma'am, suh, holding eye contact too long, or not moving aside into the gutter, while they walked on the sidewalk. He smiled slightly thinking of all the years he'd gone to her room and slept for years, only to have the tables turn. Maybe she'd needed company all those nights as well. Now, whenever he'd have a nightmare he'd just stare at the ceiling all night until he'd eventually fall back asleep. Sometimes, he would terrify women when he'd wake up in the night screaming and sweating. Not once did he tell them what he dreamt. He realized he'd never even told his own mother. He'd only told Hannah.

A week later, Henry went over to the Evans house only to be told that Hannah had gone down to the lake.

"Which lake? Paradise or Idlewild?" he asked Mrs. Evans.

"Idlewild. She's on one of those empty lots in the woods somewhere."

He drove up to the clearing and then walked the rest of the way through the trees. This plot of land, he knew well, although he hadn't been here in a while. It just reminded him of his shortcomings. The lake was nestled in the middle of the trees that were a lush green during this time of year. The leaves rustled in the breeze, making music that sounded like the falling of light rain. The place was over run with tall grass and weeds. When they were kids, they'd seen a couple of snakes here and screamed until one of them was able to kill it with a big rock or something. The water was a muted sapphire color that was rippling with the light breeze. He could see her sitting close by the wildflowers, reading a book, when she heard his steps through the grass and turned.

"I see you've healed," Hannah said, when he got close.

"I have," he said, sitting next to her on the grass.

"I could've sworn it was vanity that made you be so reclusive these past few days."

He grinned. "Ah, you missed me."

"You flatter yourself Henry."

"You should be nice to me. In fact, you're trespassing on my land."

"What do you mean *your* land?"

"Bought it when I got out of school."

"You're kidding."

"I'm serious."

"Where'd you get the money to buy this?"

He smiled. "Not exactly a Christian method, but I was a pretty good card player. I gambled my way through school. Had some money left over and thought it'd be a good investment."

"So, you just have this land sitting here?"

"I'm gonna do something with it."

He honestly had left it bare because he could never figure out what to do with it. He changed the subject as he looked down at the brown backed book. "What are you reading?" he snatched up the book before she could take it back. "Poémes d'amour," he said, looking down into her chocolate eyes. "I'm not a French student, but I believe that means 'love poems'."

"Yes, something wrong with that?"

"Nope," he said, putting his arms behind his head and laying down in the grass. "I know you women thrive on that stuff."

"And men don't thrive on love?"

"I suppose some do."

"You don't believe in love?" Hannah said incredulously.

He turned on to his side to look at her. "I believe it exists."

"Just not for you?"

"Exactly."

"Wow," she said. "Seems like a bleak existence."

"Not really." The sun was warm on his face and he laid back on the grass, taking it in.

"You really plan on sampling every woman until you're grey?"

"Yup, that was the plan."

"That's sick."

He roared with laughter. "You were never short of opinions."

"I think you're going to meet a girl that has you so sick in love you won't know what to do with yourself. I hope you pine after her."

Henry made a show of clutching his heart. "You wound me, Hannah."

"I wish I could really hurt you."

"Now, now, don't be so vile. I just healed, remember?" he said, winking at her.

She huffed and rolled her eyes.

He grew serious. "The real reason I came was to give a proper thanks for that night at the club. You really saved my ass. Don't tell anyone I said that though. I have a reputation to uphold."

"Pride will get you nowhere."

"I figured you'd say that. So I'm prepared to lay my pride aside. Since I owe you my life, I'm willing to do whatever you want. I don't take you to be one who blackmails or degrades people, so please live up to my high expectations of you."

Hannah looked shocked. "Wow, what should I say? I'm flattered Henry...This is a big deal. The mighty Henry Carrington is surrendering. I should think long and hard about this."

"Oh lord," Henry said, watching her smile. She looked natural as she had the day when she had come with the breakfast. Her brown eyes glittered with glee.

"I got it."

"Ok, so what is it? Give you my car? Money? A life?"

She almost looked wounded for a moment at that last barb before she said, "No, this is more for you than for me."

"For me?"

"Yes, I want you to stop drinking."

"What?!" He said sitting straight up.

"Yes, I think if you'd stop you'd think much clearer, you'd stop womanizing and maybe even start your own business because you'd have time to draw."

"No. What the hell does drinking have to do with anything? I just drink to have a good time." She thought he was some failure and disappointment just like his mama.

"You're drunk every other night."

"Listen, I'm a grown man and I can do what I want. It's my life. Choose something else. Choose something for yourself. Surely you must have something you want."

"Nothing I want, you can give me," she looked him in the eyes. "I thought you were stronger than that Henry. But now I know you're weak and a coward. You can't even give up your precious brandy."

His jaw tightened. "Who the hell are you to call me weak?"

She jumped slightly at his coarseness. "I've always been the only one to be honest with you. Always have. But I don't need this," she said getting up. "Obviously you have no intention of doing 'anything I asked'." She got up and started to walk away.

"Fine!" he said, getting up on his feet.

She turned around. "What did you say?"

"You heard me. I said fine. I'll do it. But that's it missy. That was a tall order. You can't ask for nothing else."

She smiled. "Do you promise you'll do it?"

"Yeah, yeah" he said, waving his hand.

"I mean it Henry."

"I gave you my word, didn't I?"

She walked back to him. "You can do this."

He didn't say anything, just looked down into her face. God, she was beautiful. If he didn't catch a grip on himself he'd kiss her right then and there.

"Thank you," she said, nervously before she headed off in the direction of home.

He watched her walk off before he sat in the grass and really contemplated what he'd just agreed to.

The next day as Henry was at work helping cut some logs to build another doghouse, he wondered what he was supposed to do for fun now. He could still go to Pete's, but he'd be too tempted to drink now. He hadn't had a drink but his head was pounding with all the sounds of hammering around him. Felt like his head was in a vice grip. It almost felt as bad as all those blows he'd gotten the last time he was at Pete's. He thought of the feel of Hannah's hands as she had tended to him. They'd felt soft despite the pain. Robert, broke his daze, throwing a bit of sawdust at him.

"Look alive!"

"What else is there to look like? I ain't dead," Henry said, smiling. He went back to sawing at the wood.

"What'cha day dreaming about? Had a wild night with Maureen?" Robert called out over the load atmosphere of men bustling about, chopping wood, and hammering.

"No," Henry said. In fact he hadn't thought about Maureen in a while. She'd only been here for a month and the girl with the sparkling brown eyes and the sassy mouth had him in knots.

"Oh, so someone new? What'd you meet her at Pete's?"

"No, it's not a girl," he lied.

"Well, then get to work my friend before the boss comes and fires our black asses."

Henry shook his head and resumed working.

After his shift he told the guys he was heading off to do some business and drove in the direction of the lake. He knew he was sweaty and grimy, but he needed some company, even if it was from Hannah. He'd always gotten sweaty at work, but never this sweaty. But, even though he felt like crap, he wasn't ready to go home just yet. When he found her, she was splashing water on her face, and then lifted her dress up past her thighs and stepped into the water. She looked like something out of a watercolor painting. He swallowed hard as his attraction swelled and he approached silently.

"Well, well, well."

Turning around cost her the grip on her dress. "Aww! Henry thanks a bunch!"

"Sorry, didn't think I'd scare you."

She composed herself and walked out from the lake. "What are you doing here?"

Now, he hadn't thought about an answer to that. "I...uh.."

She cocked an eyebrow.

"I just wanted to talk," he finally said.

Her face gave away her surprise. "Talk?"

"Yes," he said.

"About what?"

"Work." He shrugged. "Life, I suppose."

She sat down on the grass and patted the spot next to her. He looked at her for a few moments and she turned back to look at him. "Well, are you coming?"

He smiled despite himself and sat down next to her. Her hand signaled him to begin. He cleared his throat. "I haven't done this in a while...really talked to someone."

"But, you have so many friends. Everyone knows you."

"That doesn't mean anything."

She nodded her understanding. "Neither I. My only friend was Claire in France. I miss her. I named the car after her."

"You named my car after an old French woman?"

"She was a great woman."

He smiled slightly. "Well, I'm glad she was there for you. To be honest, you're the only real friend I ever had."

She froze and he wondered if he'd scared her off.

"What about Pete?"

He smirked. "Well, I guess Pete counts. He's like a father though, he probably keeps me around, cause I'm good for his business, and I help him with his ledgers. So, Miss Hannah, you're it. The only *real* friend."

"That was a long time ago," she said, coldly.

He was disappointed by her answer, but knew he deserved it. "I'm sorry about what I did. For being a jerk."

She searched his eyes. "Why are you apologizing now?"

"Cause you deserve it. Cause I hope we can be friends like we were before."

"You really wanna be my friend again?" she asked, skeptically.

He certainly wanted to be more than that, but decided against saying otherwise. "Yes."

She looked down at the grass. "Ok." It was said so faintly that he scarcely heard it. He smiled.

"Well, now that we're friends, I should tell you that I've had a long and hard day at work."

Her dimples sunk into her cheeks. "You build houses and buildings, surely you didn't expect it to be easy."

He made a face at her before responding. "I'm just tired of working for these white people who treat us like crap. I've gone to dozens of contractors trying to open my own business. None will even look at me."

"Yes, that happens here in America. The land of the free," she said sarcastically. "France can be like that too. Most people turned me down initially. They didn't think I'd be as qualified as the next white woman."

"But, at least you succeeded in what you wanted."

Her eyes bore into his. "And so will you. You've always found a way."

The words touched him deeply. He felt them wash over him and sink into the dry, cracked places in him. He knew he should move from here before he did something he'd regret.

He got up and looked down at her. "Thank you for your kind words. I'm surprised I didn't hear any sarcasm in that."

She smiled. "It can be arranged."

"I'm a bit sweaty and I suppose smelly as well."

"You said it, I didn't."

He shook his finger at her playfully and then turned to look at the lake. He began to pull his shirt out his trousers.

"What are you doing?" she asked, as he unbuttoned his shirt.

"What's it look like I'm doing? I'm going for a swim." He said, backing off the shirt and pulling the button on his trousers.

She blushed fiercely. "Henry, this is really improper."

He was down to nothing but his drawers and she looked away from him in embarrassment.

"What's improper? We used to do this all the time."

"We were kids."

"And now we're adults."

"Exactly!" she hissed. He laughed and dived into the water. Under, the world was clear, filled with bubbles algae, devoid of noise. He came back up to the surface. The water had a slight chill to it, but it felt nice after a day working under the sun.

"Come in, Hannah. You know you want to."

"I do not."

"Yes, you do," he faked a cramp and called out to her. "Hannah! I think I have a cramp come help me!"

"If you think I'm going to fall for that, then you must've lost all your good sense."

He almost sucked in water laughing. "You're right. It looks like I'm going to have to come get you myself."

He came out of the water, his feet touching the murkiness before he got to the grass.

"You wouldn't," she said, squinting her eyes.

"I would. You know I would."

He started to come for her, but she held up her hand to him. "No need to ambush me. I'm gonna come in."

"You are?"

"Yes I am."

"Are you gonna strip down?" he asked, grinning.

She folded her arms. "No, Henry."

He bowed. "Well, after you," he said.

She curtsied and before he knew it she ran and jumped into the lake.

They played in the water, racing one another, floating, playing marco polo, although he cheated almost every time and she yelled at him for it. The sunlight sparkled on the rippling water, like little stars that had been made visible by day.

"There's an opportunity to design a new hotel in town," he said to her as she floated next to him.

She dunked underneath the water and then came up in front of him, wiping at her eyes. "Are you gonna take it?"

"I don't know. Heard that some man, Dr. Kingston is running it, and he's a hard man to get to."

"Are you nervous?"

"Like hell."

"Tu peux le faire."

"What?"

"I'm sorry, I've been doing that a lot mama says. Slipping back into French," she explained. "It means 'you can do it'."

"I don't mind you speaking French. Reminds me of when you used to obsess about learning it. Plus, it's kind of sexy."

She splashed water at him. "Behave yourself."

He grinned. "You're right. I should." He did some backstrokes for a little and then swam back. "Tell me one of those poems in your book."

"Why? Won't I tempt you with my French?"

"Unlike you, I don't mind a little temptation," He winked at her.

"You need a keeper."

She recited poems for him from her book and he was mesmerized at how lyrical and smooth the French words came off her tongue. They spent the whole time in the water until the sun began to set. He offered her his coat when they emerged from the water and he saw her shivering. He did it to keep him from viewing her body that was printed out against the thin fabric of her dress. She was going to be more than a temptation. He dropped her home and then headed to his house.

"Why are you wet?" his mother asked, as he opened the door. She was by the couch knitting something Henry couldn't quite recognize.

"Went for a swim."

"By yourself?"

"With Hannah."

"Oh," his mom said, her eyes twinkling. "Did you have a good time?"

He laughed. "Yes, Mama. It was nothing. We're just friends. She's not as bad anymore. She's grown up."

"I see."

He looked at her once more. "Don't get any ideas."

"I won't," she said smiling.

And with that he headed upstairs.

The days of July seemed to melt away as he spent all his time at work and then with Hannah talking and writing letters to Dr. Kingston. Because he'd cut out the drinking, he'd spent most of the early part of the month throwing up, feeling a mix of irritation and fatigue. He'd sweat even on the days when the temperature would drop, which was common in Michigan. In fact, he'd had so many nightmares of nooses and men chasing him, that now Hannah had gone back to leaving her window open for him at nights. Most days he'd have to fight not to head straight into Pete's and chug down a beer, just for old times sake. But, he'd told Pete about his deal with Hannah, Pete agreed, and wouldn't give him anymore more booze. Pete said it was a bad business move on his part, but at least Henry was doing something good with himself. Even if he went to any of the other clubs and restaurants, he was sure someone would tell Hannah and she'd have a fit. Plus, he couldn't afford to drink every night at one of those places. Henry owed Pete some fixtures to his place, once he got himself together. July was a hard month for Henry and he and Hannah fought fiercely, mostly due to his unstable moods. Mentally, he knew that she was offering something better for him; his body just hadn't gotten the message yet.

He'd noticed a few things about her; like that she always carried the slightest smell of vanilla, that she still loved the wildflowers that grew close to the lake, and the hydrangea that could be seen around some of the residents' homes. She also loved children, and he'd see the way she'd bend down to be eye level with them when she talked to them, always saying a kind word. She started picking up money doing some of the little girls' hair, whose father's had lost their wives, and every cent she made she gave it to her mama, or bought some treats and candy for the kids. He'd call her a saint, if it wasn't for her fiery temper whenever he crossed her. Last week he'd laughed when a man in town said that he only needed women for comfort and pleasure. Hannah almost killed him for that. She talked for half an hour about the value of a woman and Henry had to apologize for his "insensitivity towards the female sex". Sometimes, he was sure that Hannah had learned this behavior from his mother, not from the mild-mannered Mrs. Evans. But, Hannah said that her mother told her that her father had been just as feisty as she. So, he supposed maybe it was in her genes. She'd probably gotten all that sweetness and innocence from her mother.

Every few days when he left for work, she'd offer to take his letters into town to be delivered. But, still there was no answer. He appreciated her way more than he let on, since they maintained their usual teasing banter with each other, and each day keeping his promise to his mother and to Pete was getting difficult. It was the last weekend in July and still he had no work prospects for the fall and winter. It was Saturday morning when he woke early and walked over to Hannah's house. She opened the door in her thin peach colored nightgown, her eyes half opened, her hair messy.

"Why are you here so early?"

"It's eight in the morning Hannah. Even your mother is out fishing already. Paris has spoiled you."

She sneered at him before opening the door to let him in. "What do you want Henry?" she asked, moving to the stove to heat some water. She went around the corner, and he could hear the pipe water and the sound of her brushing her teeth.

He sat down at the small table in the kitchen. "I came to take you out to the bookstore."

The sound of the water stopped, and she came back around wiping at her mouth. "What's the occasion?"

"Nothing. Just wanted to say thank you for all your help with the letters."

"Are you sick? You hate the bookstore."

"I don't hate it."

She raised her eyebrows. He continued, "Ok, well, I hate spending hours in there."

She smiled. "So, I should keep it short then?"

"Please," he begged.

"Ok, I'll only spend one hour," she said, winking as the kettle whistled. She turned and took it off the fire on the stove.

He sighed loudly.

"Would you like a cup of tea?"

"No, thanks. Had my coffee already."

She poured herself a cup and sat down at the table. The smell of the tea filled Henry's nostrils. "I have news to tell you...I met Mrs. Kingston the other day in town when I was delivering a letter."

He looked her up and down. "Hannah, please don't toy with me."

She chuckled. "I'm not. I ran into Pete outside the post office, and I was messing with him, and talking in French. She overheard and asked if I spoke it fluently. Vivian is very nice and she asked if I could come and tutor her children in French for the rest of the summer. Dr. Kingston speaks it, but he's very busy and has no time. Plus, his children say he's a bit too hard on them."

He smiled. "Congratulations Hannah! Did you tell your mother?"

"Not yet. I want to surprise her. The pay would help a lot around here. Our mamas can't spend all their days cooking and sewing for people."

"No, they can't," he said, looking down at the table and scratching at the wood with his index finger.

She touched his hand gently and he stilled. "There's more."

He looked up at her waiting to hear the news as she smiled. She continued, "I explained to Mrs. Kingston that I'd been delivering letters for weeks to her husband concerning the development project. I gave her your name and I took one of your sketches and showed it to her."

He could feel his heart thumping with excitement.

"I didn't think she'd listen to me. But she assured me that she'd talk to her husband."

Henry beamed and jumped out the chair.

"Don't get too worked up," she said, although she was smiling and laughing at his excitement.

He picked her up out of the chair and gave her a big kiss on her cheek. "Spend all the time you want at the bookstore, ok?"

She looked at him wide eyed. "Ok," she whispered.

He hadn't intended to kiss her although he wished he could do it again. Her cheek had been so soft that he wondered what her lips and the rest of her felt like. "Go wash up. I'll meet you outside whenever you're ready."

She nodded silently before placing the cup in the sink and strolling up the stairs. He moved to the sink and washed the cup for her before heading outside. He didn't know why just a simple kiss on the cheek had riveted him. But, still he couldn't stop having the jittery feeling that little boys feel when they have their first girlfriend. He remembered the disaster that had ensued when Hannah had found out he had dumped her for Maureen. He knew that Hannah had felt that maybe it was because Maureen had been lighter and came from a more affluent family. Most of the people in Idlewild that had come up during the time their mamas had moved them up, had come from middle class or wealthy families, just looking to escape segregation and Jim Crow. Some though, once they got there they had looked their noses down at the others who were darker hued. He remembered the comments Mrs. Evans and Hannah had gotten, and Henry's mother had ripped into anyone who had something bad to say. Hannah had suffered badly at school, and Henry had gotten by just because his skin was a tanned color instead of the dark chocolate, velvet soft skin Hannah had. He'd always looked more at the lighter women to be honest. They'd offered him variety not just in skin tone, but they had a variety of eye colors, hazel, green and grey, and usually they were well connected in society. But, as Hannah walked out the house in her white blouse and mint green skirt, he saw the evenness of her skin and the way her brown eyes shined.

He forced himself to remain calm as she walked to the car and hopped in. She looked at him from the passenger seat.

"Is something wrong?" she asked.

"No," he said, getting into the car. "Just lost in thought." He started the car and headed towards town.

On the way they talked about her new job. She would start in about a weeks time, and he was happy that at least she wouldn't be bored around the house anymore. When they got to the bookstore, the smell of old paper met him. Mr. Cooper was shocked to see him of course, and commented on how this was just like old times. Henry entertained Hannah by helping her pick out books. He even found some on architecture and decided to get those too. She'd kept fighting him on every new book he recommended, saying that she couldn't ask him to spend so much on her, in which he ignored her and kept telling Mr. Cooper to add it to the tab.

Hannah was arguing that she'd already ran the bill up to five dollars when Henry heard the door chime and Jeffrey Olson walked in. Hannah turned her back to the bookshelf pretending not to notice him. Henry observed her and gave Olsen a cool glare. Olsen ignored him and turned his attention to Hannah.

"Miss Evans."

She turned around to face him, giving him a sweet smile. "Mr. Olsen."

"Remember, I told you last time you could call me Jeffrey."

"Jeffrey."

"I haven't seen you in a while. I wondered if you had left off to Europe again."

"No. I'm still here."

Olsen looked at Henry before saying, "So, have you decided when you'll go with me to dinner?"

She turned away out of embarrassment. "I'm not sure."

"Not sure *when* or *if* you will go with me?"

She turned around to face him. "If."

"Ahh, I see." His light colored face was flushed with embarrassment before he turned a stony look at Henry. "I didn't think you'd be the type to fall for Carrington's schemes."

"Excuse me?" Henry and Hannah said at the time.

"I didn't take you for the type to be whoring around with Carrington. You seemed better than that."

Henry clenched his fists and moved forward. Hannah reached out her hand and held him back. "Henry, please," she said, looking at him, her eyes pleading with him to maintain his composure. Henry relaxed back, keeping his eye on Olsen. He wanted to knock him so hard in the jaw, that he couldn't open that mouth for days. Hannah cleared her throat and stepped forward towards Olsen. "For your information, you're right, 'I'm not *whoring* around' with Henry. He's a friend," she said, gritting her teeth.

"My apologies," he said, looking quite chastised.

"I expected better than that *Mr. Olsen*. I thought you were a gentleman."

She tried moving from him, but he held her arm and Henry moved forward again, to which Hannah yelled, "Henry! It's ok. I can handle it."

"Let go of her Olsen, or I swear I'll kill you," Henry said.

Olsen looked at Henry. "I helped you that night when you were knocked out. You touch me and I'll make sure your Mammy's house is gone tomorrow." Olsen turned back to Hannah. "You should give me the chance to explain."

"You've angered me enough," she said. She tried to move again, but his grip tightened. She looked into his eyes. "Let go." He made no move.

"Olsen, I think you better get out of my shop now," Mr. Cooper said, leveling his rifle at him. "I don't owe you no money, so no use in threatening me."

He loosened his grip and Hannah snatched her hand away. Olsen took one last look at her before leaving.

"That man is bad news," Mr. Cooper said. "Stay clear of him."

"I've been warned before," she said, looking at Henry. "I'm sorry Henry, I think we should go."

Henry closed his eyes and tried to calm himself, as he heard the door chime and watched Hannah walked out. He told Mr. Cooper not to bother wrapping the books and just put them in a box, paid him the bill, and walked out of the store. Hannah was leaning against the black car, her head down, looking at her feet. He opened the car for her, when he got in he looked at her as she sat quietly and looked out the window.

"Are you alright?" he asked.

"I've never had anyone call me a whore. That was humiliating."

"I'm sorry."

She swallowed, wiped at her eyes and squared her shoulders. "I'll be fine."

He started the car and began to drive away from town. "Who cares about his opinion? Or anyone else's for that matter? You know who you are."

She turned to him now. "What did he mean about taking away your mama's house?"

Henry sighed loudly. Hannah shouldn't have found out about that. He'd been such an idiot before and he wasn't sure he was ready for her to know just how much of one he was. It would be best to tell her the truth since she was too smart to believe a lie. "When I came out of college I had such a swelled head-"

"That hasn't changed," she said, before looking at his annoyance. "Sorry, continue please."

"Thank you. As I was saying, I was an idiot. I was doing some gambling and Olsen betted the property tax to the house and the deed. I was overconfident and agreed. As you can see I lost."

Hannah shook her head. "How much do still you owe him?"

"Five hundred."

Her eyes widened.

"Before you give me the verbal lashing that I deserve, I should tell you that I know I was stupid and I've been paying him regularly. Olsen just did that to embarrass me."

She opened her mouth to say something and Henry continued, "No, mama doesn't know and I'd like for it to stay that way. She already thinks I'm the biggest screwup."

Hannah looked at him, her features softening. "Henry, your mother doesn't think that. She loves you."

"I know she does, but I've made nothing out of my life. Not like my pa did."

"You went to college and graduated with good grades."

"And drank and whored around since I've come home. It's my fault I can't find any good work."

She looked at him and smiled. "That's gonna change. Sobering up did you some good."

He smiled faintly. "Yeah, I suppose it did," he said, paying more attention to the road now. "You wanna go riding horses or to the skating rink?" he asked.

"No, I'd rather go to the lake."

She nodded and they drove in silence until he saw the white ash trees and parked. He got out of the car and hurried to the passenger side and opened the door for her.

"I know you can do it yourself, 20th century woman."

"Good, I'm glad you remembered, but thanks."

They both made the trek through the woods to the lake. Both of them looked out at the water, the tall grass brushing against their calves. "You gotta give me some suggestions for this land."

"Well, you could build a mansion on this land and still have plenty left over."

"A house?"

"Yes, why not?"

"A small cabin would do just fine."

"A cabin? Henry, surely you don't intend on bringing a wife, much less a family inside a cabin."

He chuckled. "A wife and family."

"Yes, you'll have to settle down some day. I'm sure that Maureen will be pleased if you built her a nice house. She's probably having a fit that you've been sitting on this land for years."

"Maureen doesn't know about this land. No one does."

She looked confused. "Why wouldn't you tell her?"

"Cause then she'd ask me to build her a house or something."

Her eyes studied him for a little. "But, you've been with her for years."

He walked closer to her. "Maureen is...not the girl that I'd spend the rest of my life with."

"*Non?*"

"I'm not in love with her."

"You don't believe in love."

"I think I've changed my mind," he said. She lifted her eyebrows like she always did involuntary. He cleared his throat and clarified. "All your French poems that you've read to me make me think that maybe it will happen for me someday."

"Maureen will be hurt."

"Maureen will be fine. I hear she's already on some guy's arm."

"She's hurting. Women are different. She's probably spent most of her life waiting for you to marry her."

"Are you attempting to make me feel guilty?"

"No," she said, smiling softly. "Just warning you that a woman's heart is fragile. You shouldn't tamper with it."

He looked ahead at the lake. "Was there anyone in France that promised you love and houses?"

She chuckled. "Oh, God no. They were some who promised me one night. I didn't take them up on their offers."

"Smart girl."

She turned to face him. "What's wrong with you men? All you want is just a sexual fantasy and then you're done."

For the first time he felt a tinge of embarrassment for the way he'd been in and out of beds. "Some of us take longer to grow up than others. I'm finally starting to, I think."

"I'm glad some sense is finally starting to hit you," she started to walk around, looking at the trees, green and alive.

He was sure something else was hitting him too. "Hannah..."

"Yes," she said, and he was taken a back again at her beauty. He wanted to lean in and kiss her properly this time. This morning hadn't been enough.

Pete's and his mother's words rand in his ears. "Um...what kind of house would a woman want? If I were to build something for a wife and family?"

"I can't speak for every woman out there."

"Just tell me."

She let out a breath and looked around. "I'd want a big house painted a light blue with a front and back porch. Even though I know shoveling the snow is horrible. I just like sitting out on the porch in the summer. I'd also want a couple of rooms because I want lots of babies."

"Lots?"

"*Oui, beaucoup*," she said, smiling. "I'd want a fireplace, a shower and a claw foot tub like the one in Paris. And a big dining table so that everyone can fit when we have a family dinner."

"Is that all?"

"Yes, I think so. Is that too much?"

"Not for the woman who's been waiting her whole life for a husband and fainting from French poetry."

She pinched him.

"You're so violent," he said, playfully.

"When you find the woman you will marry I'm sure she'll have an even longer list."

"This was just a hypothetical thing. Who said I'll marry?"

"Oh, I'm hoping for it."

"You are?" he said, surprised.

"Yes, I'm hoping that one girl will tame you. Make you go out of your mind."

"You're wishing bad things."

"It's not a bad thing. It will change you," she said, and then she cleared her throat. "Well since you don't plan on marrying, maybe you should build a bed and breakfast. Make some money. You'd still have room to build and your cabin and maybe even a small restaurant."

That wouldn't be such a bad idea and Henry mulled over it. "It would bring in some income in case things don't work out with

Dr. Kingston. But, then again I'm in the hole and can't afford to build anything right now."

"You have to have some faith Henry."

"Faith in what?"

"Yourself. In God."

Henry rolled his eyes. She rolled her eyes back at him. "I suppose I'll have to do it for you then," she said.

The wind was blowing lightly and he smelled her vanilla scent wafting in the air. He swallowed and looked up at the sky.

"I should probably get you home now," he said. If he didn't he couldn't tell what he'd say or do.

"Ok."

They started to walk back to the car when she looked over to him. "Henry, do you think that someday a man will actually fall in love with me?"

He knew he should just tell her that he was already in danger of doing just that, but the Lothario in him was not willing to surrender yet. "I don't think you'll have a problem with winning a man's heart. I think the problem will be for him to win yours."

"That's a sweet thing to say."

"Just the truth."

She looked ahead in deep thought. "Does it make me common to actually want a family?" she asked.

"Hannah, I don't think you'll ever be common."

"Is that an insult or compliment?"

"Compliment. You 20th century women need to learn how to take one."

Her sweet smile and the curve of her lips were continuing to play with his mind. "Come on," he said. "Let's get you home."

They stayed silent most of the way home and he wondered how after only two months back, she had bulldozed into his heart. She took up most of the spaces in his mind that he thought had been filled before. He'd been infatuated before by the clicks a woman's heels made, or the way she danced, but never had the whole woman filled him. He wanted to build her that house and even give her those kids. What the hell was happening to him? He'd always said that he'd sample women until he was old and now he couldn't even look at someone without thinking of Hannah's eyes, her lips or the way her breasts, hips, and bottom tempted him. Every girl he thought about now paled in comparison to the way she would verbally spar with him, and still be gentle enough to console him the next moment. She only said a goodbye to him as he pulled up to her house and let herself out. As we watched her go inside the house he vowed that no matter how hard it would be; he would have to keep his distance. He didn't want to cause her pain and maybe this was just a phase because he hadn't been with her yet, but he couldn't do that because she wasn't his and would most likely never be.

"So when are you coming back to Pete's?" Robert asked on Monday at work as the other men milled around cutting, hammering, spitting, and swearing.

"Not sure," Henry said, continuing the work on the roof.

"What the hell do you mean you're not sure? You know you're the life of the party."

"Well, now you can take my place."

"There's someone else taking your place with Maureen too."

He looked up at Robert waiting to hear the rest.

"She's been asking for you and complaining that you're too busy messing around with Hannah from school?"

Henry rolled his eyes. "Jealous female. I'm not sleeping with Hannah."

"I haven't gotten to see her myself, since you've got her locked up most of the time, but I heard she looks sweet now. You sure you haven't yet?"

"No," he said, as he gritted his teeth. "We've just been hanging out. We've been neighbors all our lives man."

"We all went to high school together and you didn't talk to her for the longest time."

"Look, we're just friends."

Robert started hammering again. "Someone is defensive. Anyways, I meant to tell you that Maureen has been on some businessman's arm lately. Says you've been ignoring her."

"She's a grown woman. She can do what she wants."

Robert looked at him, but he flashed him a dark look that asked for no more questions and they both went back to work.

The next Monday, Hannah started working for Dr. Kingston and every evening she'd come home telling him stories about the family. The kids were really shy at first, but they'd loosened up to her after the first week. She said that Dr. Kingston always maintained his distance, but had complimented her on her knowledge of the language and literature. She never brought up whether his wife had given him those sketches and Henry decided not to press her on information and get disappointed.

The summer was starting to wrap up, it was already the end of August and soon all the tourists would head out. He was feeling much better these days. The alcohol had made it out his system and he'd stopped feeling so tired and nauseous and sweating all the time. Hannah was also happy that he'd stopped snapping and that his nightmares had lessened, even though sometimes he faked one so he could sleep in her room.

Henry was at work one day when he heard whistling and hooting. Robert dragged him out to see what the fuss was about. Hannah. He could see her in a red dress with a matching hat, walking alongside another worker named Mosley.

Robert whistled through his teeth. "Who is that?" he asked.

"Hannah."

"What?!" Robert said, looking back at Hannah.

Mosley called out. "Carrington! Someone's here to see you."

Henry hurried down to meet them before he could hear one of the men say something, least of all Robert. The closer he got to her was the more he thought of the way she teased him and he wanted to just kiss her and... He needed to quiet his thoughts right now. Her eyes were wide and she bit on her bottom lip nervously.

"Come on, let's go somewhere more private," Henry said to her. He nodded a thanks to Mosley, and gently pulled Hannah off to the side. "What are you doing here?" he asked her softly.

"I'm so sorry. This was a bad idea. I...just..."

"Don't be embarrassed. Is everything ok?"

She grinned and he liked the way her red lipstick looked. "Ok, well I should tell you that I opened some mail for you."

"What?"

She raised her hand. "I'm sorry. Mrs. Kingston gave me a letter for you and I got excited and I couldn't resist."

"Hannah," he said, shaking his head.

"I know, I know, I'm sorry. But in one minute you're gonna love me." She stuck out the letter.

He took it from her, his heart thumping as he read,

Mr. Carrington, I've received your letters and along with your sketch as well as your recommendation by Miss Evans, I'd like to meet with you this Monday morning at nine to discuss the plans for development.

Dr. Claude Kingston

Henry swallowed before speaking. "Wow," was the only word he could manage to say.

"Henry, this is it. I'm so proud of you,' she said, before hugging him.

Her body felt warm against his and as she pulled away he looked down into her brown eyes. "Thank you, Hannah."

She smiled softly and the air felt thick and humid all of a sudden as they continued looking at each other.

Robert came up to them. "Hannah! Long time, no see."

Hannah looked at him, recognition hitting her face. "Robbie Taylor."

"In the flesh," he said, taking her hand and kissing it. Henry wanted to throttle him. "That's what they do in France, right?"

Hannah laughed. "*Oui.*"

"So has Henry invited you to Pete's for some dancing?" Robert asked, her still holding her hand.

"That's not really Hannah's type of place."

"Why not?" Hannah said, and Henry stared. "It sounds fun."

"Well, then it's settled. Henry can bring you at nine."

Henry stood there stammering. "You sure you want to go?"

Hannah smiled. "Absolutely."

"Ok," he said, not knowing what to do next.

"Well, I should probably head on back home," Hannah said, nodding politely at Robert. "I'll be ready at eight thirty," she said to Henry before leaving, her red dress accentuating her small waist.

Henry watched her walk off.

"You're in love with that girl."

Henry turned around to face Robert. "Shut up," Henry said, walking off to his post.

Robert followed him. "Damn, you really are in love with her."

"Look, she's my friend. Nothing more."

"Yeah, she's your friend. But, both of you want more than that. A blind man can see that."

Henry sighed. "She doesn't need someone like me. I got nothing to give her."

"Man, you underrate yourself. Plus, what about the proposal you gave those businessmen? It might go through."

Henry didn't want anyone to know yet that he'd gotten through to Dr. Kingston. He sighed. "You think so?"

"Yeah. And when it does, you gotta make me a partner," Robert said, slapping him on the back.

Henry grinned. "So you can send me to the poor house?"

"Nope, so I can make things fun and check out the secretary."

Both of them laughed as they headed back to work. The rest of the day at work Henry was in a good mood and worked with fervor. He cut more wood than anyone and finished off one side of a doghouse they were working on. When work ended at six he raced out from the site and headed home. He got home and showered and put on a clean white shirt, his trousers, and suspenders. Combing through his hair and putting on some cologne, he breathed deeply and headed out to Hannah's house. As he neared he wondered if he should've brought her something, but then he remembered that Hannah was supposed to be his friend, not his woman. He knocked on Hannah's door and she opened the door. She was wearing a sapphire colored dress and her hair was curled at the ends.

"Well, look at you," he said, definitely wishing that he had those flowers now.

"Do I look alright?"

"You look great."

"Thank you. You look handsome," she said, blushing.

Mrs. Evans came and broke the silence. "Well, you two git. And Henry, take care of my girl."

He smiled. "I will Mrs. Evans."

She yelled out, "Keep your hands to yourself Henry!"

Hannah covered her face in embarrassment and Henry laughed. "Understood, Mrs. Evans!" he yelled back.

They both went to the car and Henry started to drive down the road. Henry hadn't experienced this nervousness since he was a boy. She looked gorgeous.

"Nervous?" he asked her.

She smiled softly. "A little."

"You'll be fine," Henry said. He hoped he'd be fine too.

"I hope so..." she said softly, looking out the window.

He touched one of her hands and rubbed it softly with his thumb. "Just have fun tonight. Don't think so much."

She smiled. "Ok."

He moved his hand in order to calm himself. The night air was cool and the place normally would've been pitch dark if it hadn't been for the lights from the clubs and the dozens of cars lined up to get to the different clubs. "How's work?" he asked.

"Good, but the summer is just about over and the family will leave. I need work. I want to make things easier on Mama and the winter is coming."

Henry groaned. "I hate the winters here."

"We're both on the same page."

"I'll help you and your mother. Chop wood, anything you two need."

"Henry, I can chop wood."

"I know you can, just like you can open the door, get me a job and save me from getting my head caved in." She smirked, and he couldn't help but smile too. "I just want to do it for you, Hannah, can't you just accept that?"

She let a breath out. "I'm used to doing things for myself."

"I know."

"I guess I can let you do nice things for me."

"Good," he said, smiling.

He could see the lights from Pete's in the distance. Henry parked the car, then turned to her and squeezed her hand. "Just let it all go tonight. Just have fun."

Hannah smiled softly and moved to open the door. Henry gently touched her arm.

"Come on, please let me open it for you? I want to at least be some sort of a gentleman tonight."

Hannah laughed and he went over and opened her door, making a show of bowing and pulling her up by her hand.

"I think you deserve the royal treatment," Henry said.

"Why, thank you. Never had the royal treatment before."

Henry's eyes grew serious as he looked into hers. "Well I'm happy to be at your service."

Henry could see her shaking just a bit and he had to remind himself to slow down; she wasn't used to this stuff.

"Come on," he whispered softly.

They walked into Pete's and as usual, people were buzzing around and the place was alive with dancers. Robert found them quickly. He was in his usual black pants with his black suspenders, the black shoes with the white tips. Henry called him a penguin when he dressed like that, but even Henry had to admit he looked sharp.

"Hey! I was wondering if you two were gonna be a couple of no shows."

Hannah smiled. "Robbie, I wouldn't have missed this for the world."

"Well, good," he said with surprise. Henry was surprised too. "Hannah you want to jitterbug?" Hannah looked at Henry. Henry wanted to throttle Robbie for getting the first dance with her, but he smiled gently. "Have fun."

Robbie grabbed her hand and led her out to the dance floor. They started moving to the sounds of the big band music and Henry watched as Hannah moved effortlessly with Robbie. Henry didn't even know Hannah could dance. Robbie swung her across the dance floor, threw her effortlessly over his shoulder and she stayed in stride. He watched as Hannah swayed her hips and laughed with glee as Robbie twirled her.

"You gonna let him snatch your girl away like that?" Pete teased him.

"She was free to dance with whoever she wanted to."

"Yeah, but don't let her pass the night away without dancing with you."

Henry looked at Pete, and then back at Robbie and Hannah.

Pete smiled at him knowingly and Henry smiled back. "Stop looking at me like that old man."

"I ain't giving you a funny look," Pete said, smirking.

Henry rested his elbows on the bar. "I got a meeting with Dr. Kingston."

"You're serious?"

"Of course I am."

"Well, hot damn!" Pete said, letting out a loud laugh. He moved to pour him a drink and then retracted. "Oh, yes, I forgot your lady love has stolen you away from me."

Henry laughed and turned back around to see Robbie and Hannah finishing their dance. Hannah was smiling and Henry walked over.

"Can I cut in?"

Hannah looked caught off guard, and Robbie smiled knowingly. "No problem."

The music changed to something slower and Henry extended his hand. Hannah took it nervously and he pulled her in closer, beginning to sway.

"I had no idea you knew how to dance like that. I didn't expect you to know how to dance at all."

She smiled shyly. "The gardener was a young guy and he would sneak in lessons with me in turn for English lessons."

"Did he promise you one night?"

Hannah laughed. "No. He was very much in love with the maid. They eloped."

Henry could smell the warmness of her vanilla perfume. "He taught you well."

"Thank you," she said.

A couple next to them began to kiss and Hannah looked away and caught his gaze before looking at the floor.

He raised her chin. "What's wrong?"

She looked up at him, her eyes watering. "You shouldn't look at me like that."

"Like what?"

Her brown eyes were serious. "Henry, I turned down many men's offers for one night. I won't accept yours."

Even though goose bumps had begun to rise on his skin, he still held her as they swayed to the music. "I know."

She looked away from him.

"Do you want to leave?" he asked.

She nodded slowly and he took her hand, leading her out the club. Robert stopped them.

"Hey, you're leaving so soon? What's wrong?" he asked, looking at Hannah.

"It's fine," Henry said. "She just needs some fresh air. I'll see you tomorrow Rob," he said before leaving.

They walked in silence and she didn't protest when he opened her door for her. He got in and began to drive home over the sound of his thumping heart. He felt numb as he drove. She didn't want someone like him.

They pulled close to the house and as they got out the car, she whispered, "I'm so sorry I ruined the night."

"What? You didn't ruin it...I did. I should've known you wouldn't want someone like me."

"Someone like you..?" she said quizzically.

"I'm messed up. You want some clean cut guy, probably with money and I'm none of those things."

She looked at him. "What would make you think I'd want that?"

He took in her face in the moonlight and the way her hair was blowing softly in the breeze. "That's what you deserve."

She blushed and looked down. "Henry there's nothing wrong with you...I'm just not going to let you toy with me."

"Who said that's what I wanted?"

"You don't love me and to be honest, I loved you for years. But you never cared then, and you don't care for me now. You just want me. But you don't love me."

Henry released a breath he wasn't even aware he was holding. Then he began to chuckle and laugh at himself. Evidently Hannah didn't understand the humor and began to walk off.

"Wait!" Henry said going after her and twirling her around.

"I didn't need you to humiliate me, Henry," she said, trying to fight him off.

"No, no, no, I was laughing at myself. I thought I was the last person you'd want, let alone love."

She looked skeptically into his eyes and he touched her soft cheek and continued. "I haven't been able to think about anyone but you. You've been turning me inside out."

"I…" Hannah said stumbling for words. She looked at him with apprehension.

He smiled and put a finger under her chin. "I mean it Hannah," he said, before lightly brushing his lips against hers. She started to move away and he held her.

"Stay. Stay here. With me," he whispered, before kissing her again. This was much different than the kiss they had nearly a decade ago. Her lips were too soft and the madness he thought would stop once he tasted her, only grew more. He'd want her forever. To kiss her this way, to feel the shyness in her touch. All that mattered were her lips and the way her body felt underneath his hands. She broke the kiss and stood there with her eyes closed for a few moments. When she opened them, he was looking down at her and she looked down at the ground.

"I'm rusty," she whispered. "I don't know if I did that right."

Henry chuckled. "You were perfect."

She put a hand on his chest. "Thank you for that. But, Henry I can't let you do that again."

"Why not? I thought you felt the same way."

"Henry, you don't understand," she said, backing away slightly. "I told you, I feel something for you much greater than what you feel for me. You want passion. I want love."

"Hannah," he said, reaching for her hand. She stepped back. "What if we could have both?"

She smiled softly. "Surely, you don't believe that a kiss will convince me that you love me?"

"Maybe," he said.

"No, Henry," she said, shaking her head. "How many women have you kissed? How many have you slept with? That didn't make you love them and that won't make you love me."

"What if I love you already?"

She laughed now and he felt his offense begin to rise. "What if I don't believe you?" she countered.

He couldn't believe this. The first woman he was even uttering the words "love" to and she was laughing right in his face. "What would convince you?"

She threw up her arms. "I don't know, I don't know." She bit her lip.

"You know I'm going to convince you, right?"

She walked close to him now and put her hand on his cheek. "I'm going to try to resist you," she whispered.

"I know," he whispered back.

She smiled. "I trust that you'll be creative."

He smiled back. "I won't disappoint you."

She nodded.

He tipped her chin once more and kissed her softly before she could refuse. "Good night Hannah."

"Good night Henry."

He watched her walk over to her door and she took one last look at him standing there, everything in his stance and eyes pleading with her to reconsider. She went in and closed the door.

The sound of frying food and bacon woke him and Henry sluggishly got out of bed. He looked out his window to see that the sun was rising in the horizon, filling the sky with pinks, yellows, and oranges against the blue sky. He showered and put on a clean shirt and trousers before going down stairs. His mama was sitting on the red plush chair sewing some shirts.

"Mornin' Mama," he said, giving her a peck on the cheek and sitting down on the other chair.

She watched him for a while. "Well, ain't you gonna eat?"

He smiled. "Not yet."

"Your food is gonna get cold."

He looked at her, holding his head in his hands. "I should be making you breakfast. You got too much on your shoulders."

She looked up from her sewing. "Henry, you ain't drunk, is you?"

He laughed. "No, Mama. I'm just thinking that I'll wake up from now on and make breakfast for you."

She put down her needlework now. "Come on, tell me what's going on. You didn't get yourself into no trouble, did you?"

He shook his head. "I don't know, maybe."

Bracing herself, she sat back on the chair. "Explain."

He imitated her movement. "I think I'm in love with Hannah."

His Mama looked at him wide eyed and then gave a hoop of excitement. "Yes! I knew it! I done told Mae that it was coming soon! Henry I gotta go tell her," she said, getting out of her chair.

"Whoa," he said, easing his mother back into her chair. "Mama, it's not that simple."

"What?" she asked.

"Hannah turned me down."

His mama gave him a confused look. "She's in love with someone else?"

"No. She loves me too...she just doesn't believe I *actually* love her. Seems my reputation has caught up with me."

She touched her hands to his. "You can't blame her."

"I don't," he said, putting his hand over hers and patting it gently. "I blame myself."

"It will work out."

"Yes, once I figure out how to convince her."

His mama smiled softly. He pulled the letter from his pocket. "Mama, there's something else. I got a job offer. I have a meeting on Monday."

"What?"

"Sorry, I didn't tell you earlier. I wanted to wait. But, I guess this is a good time. They're looking for an architect to help build a new hotel."

"They want you to build it?" she asked excitedly.

"Well, I have that meeting to see if the man in charge will put me over the project."

"My goodness! All this good news in one day!"

He smiled as she got up and went to the kitchen. She began sharing food and then put it down on the table. "Eat," she ordered. "And then get yourself out there and buy a suit for that meeting."

He laughed. "Hannah gets that bossiness from you and Mrs. Evans, I swear."

"Well, Mae and I pretty much raised her," she said, getting her needlework and then joining him at the kitchen table.

Henry started to dig into the grits and bacon. "I wasn't done."

His mama looked up to face him. "I bought some land a little while back. When I came home from school. Had planned on building something big there someday, but now I think I'll build a house for Hannah and I."

Now, she dropped her needlework on the ground. She shook her head. "I oughta take a switch to you for not tellin' me bout this land, but I'm jus' too excited now."

She picked back up her needlework. "Mae and I have to get to work on Hannah's wedding dress, and maybe we can see about making you a tux, I-"

"Mama," he said, cutting her off. "I don't mind you telling Mrs. Evans, partly because I know you will anyway. But, please don't meddle in this. Let Hannah and I work this out."

"But-"

"Mama, don't tell Hannah any of this. Don't start measuring her for that wedding gown and don't pressure her to take me. I want her to make up her own mind."

She sighed and resumed her sewing. "Ok, but you better not let me down. Been waitin' for dis for years. I want to see my grandbabies."

He smiled. "Oh, lord. I wouldn't want to face your wrath if I mess this up."

"No you don't," she said, cutting her eyes after him.

He finished up the rest of his food and then washed up the plates, gave his Mama a kiss and went to the door. "You can go next door now. I know you've been just itching for me to leave."

She laughed. "Go on! Git!" she yelled playfully, and he went out the door and to his car, driving to town. Since it was still an early Saturday morning, he stopped by Pete's knowing that he was probably in there, shining glasses and mopping floors, since he wouldn't pay no one to do it for him.

He knocked at the door and he heard Pete's voice, "We closed until 5 pm!"

"It's Henry, old man!"

The door opened and Henry stepped inside. "Watch where you steppin' boy before you dirty my clean floors."

Henry smirked. "Please," he said, dismissing him. "I need your help."

"For what?"

"Got that meeting Monday. Need help picking out a suit."

Pete laughed. "Ain't you supposed to ask your lady love to help you with that?"

"Don't want to bother her. Hannah has done more than enough for me. I want her to sleep in."

"You tell her you love her yet?"

Henry nodded. "As a matter of fact, I did, last night."

Pete looked at Henry's tight face. "I take it things didn't go well."

"Just not as I expected. I got a lot to prove to her."

Pete sat down on one of the barstools. "And getting this job is phase one."

"Maybe."

He clapped his hands and got up. "Ok, I'm comin' but you gotta do my ledgers for me later."

"Deal."

After a frustrating hour, Henry had settled on a simple tailored brown suit. The tailor, Mr. Lewis said that it wouldn't be flashy, but practical. Henry and Pete took his word for it. As he drove back home he saw that Hannah was outside on her porch sweeping and he pulled up to her house.

"Hey you," he said, coming out of the car.

With her hair pulled back, he could see her features fully. She looked almost shy before she squared her shoulders back. "Hello."

"I just came back from town. I got a suit for the meeting."

She smiled. "That's good. I'll see it on Monday," she went back to sweeping.

"Maybe I can give you a lift to work that day."

She looked up, nodded, and then continued her work.

"Is something wrong?" he asked, moving closer to her.

"No," she said, not meeting his eyes.

"Hannah?"

She looked up at him. "Everything is fine."

"Is it because of last night?"

"Oh God, no."

He let out a sigh of relief. "So I still have my chance to convince you?"

Her eyes gleamed. "Yes, *if* you can."

"Will you tell me what's bothering you?" He said, reaching for her hand.

She held his hand and his gaze. "No."

"That's not comforting. But I suppose that you've got whatever it is under control."

Those brown eyes wouldn't meet his. "I'll let you know if I need your help."

He nodded and then decided to change the topic. "Do you want to go for a swim?"

"Not if it's a ploy to get me undressed."

He smiled. "Are you a mind reader?" She shot him a dirty look and continued sweeping. "Contrary to what you may believe, I don't always have bad intentions. I just want you to have some time to relax. I need it too. Pretty nervous about this meeting."

The brushing sounds of her sweeping continued. She stopped for a moment, her hand resting on the end of the broom. "I guess I could go swimming."

He moved closer to her and leaned forward; close enough to almost brush his lips against hers. "Do you guess or do you want to come with me?"

"Our mamas are inside."

He pulled back slightly. "I wouldn't want them to get too excited."

Hannah smiled. "No, we wouldn't want that. They've been speaking in hushed tones all morning," she said, putting her hand on her hip. "Explain yourself."

He threw his hands up in surrender. "I may have told Mama some stuff."

The sound of the broom dropping filled the air. "Henry! Goodness!" Her eyes were flashing with anger. "They're probably in there sketching my wedding dress and naming our children."

He laughed. "That's exactly what they're doing."

She hit his chest. "This isn't funny."

He sat down on the bench. "You have to admit that it kinda is." She folded her arms. "Hannah, they've been waiting all their lives to do this."

"But, I never said I would marry you."

He folded his arms. "You're stubborn, but I am too, and I've already made up my mind to convince you to marry me, despite all your kicking and screaming."

"Am I supposed to fall into your arms and beg you to make an honest woman out of me?"

"Nope. I realize that it wouldn't be as satisfying if you did that."

She raised her chin and looked at him suspiciously. He stood in front of her and met her eyes. "I want to know that that same mouth that turned me down, would be sighing with pleasure on our wedding night." She looked at him wide eyed and he bent and placed a kiss on her lips.

Her eyes were still wide with surprise, "I thought I told you not to kiss me."

He ran a thumb over her bottom lip. "I couldn't resist."

She looked at him. "Tu n'es pas bon."

He smiled. "You shouldn't speak French if you want me to stop kissing you."

She pushed him away playfully. "I'm not going swimming with you anymore."

He stuck out his bottom lip. "Why not?"

"Exactly what I said a moment ago. You're trouble."

He smiled. "Well, coming from you, that might be a good thing."

"Go home."

"As you wish," he said, putting on his hat and winking at her. He headed back to his car and opened the door. "I'll be here Monday morning, bright and early."

She nodded and he drove off smiling.

Sunday, he actually got up and made an effort to get dressed for church at Tabernacle AME. When he came downstairs, his mother was shocked and that didn't measure up to the faces of Mrs. Evans, Hannah, and the rest of the congregation when he walked inside the church later. The church had wooden ceiling beams that were beautiful, Henry thought as he looked up. As he sat in the pew next to Hannah, he leaned over and whispered to her, "How long do you think it will be before everyone stops staring?"

"A couple of weeks. But, it looks like you've got a few admirers," she said, pointing to some girls who were smiling in his direction.

"Doesn't matter," he said, looking at her.

Hannah turned back her attention to the preacher. "Behave," she whispered.

"I'm trying. I forget sometimes that I'm in the house of God."

She smiled, still keeping her eyes on the preacher and he followed suit. The sermon wasn't so bad. Rev. Washington preached on Jacob wrestling with God and how each of us must confront who we are and make the decision to change. After the service, Hannah and both of their mothers greeted people around the church. The members ambushed him, begging him to come back next week, and give his heart to the Lord. He saw the looks of amusement Hannah gave him every so often as she remained on the outskirts.

"Henry, do you promise to come next week? Pastor is continuing the message on Jacob."

He looked over the old woman's head and saw a guy approach Hannah. He was talking to her.

"Do you promise?" he heard again and he looked down.

"Uh, yeah."

She smiled underneath her wide powder blue hat that matched her church suit. "See you next week," she said, walking away and Henry groaned realizing what he'd just gotten himself into. The guy left from Hannah's side and Hannah turned her attention to Henry approaching.

"I see I'm not the only one with admirers."

She smiled at him underneath her modern brown hat. "Green with envy, I see."

"I have no reason to be jealous."

"Really?" she said, inquisitively.

"Nope," he said. "I worked with him once a little over a year ago."

"And?"

"He's not your type." She raised an eyebrow and he continued. "He's not very honest. Lies about how much work he's done. No telling what else he'd lie about." She looked over at the guy and then back at Henry. "I know you can tolerate many things, because you put up with me. But lying ain't one of them."

She pursed her lips. "That's true...And you're not just saying this to look better in my eyes, are you?"

"Of course not, that would be lying wouldn't it?"

She smiled. "So how did you like the sermon?"

"Not as bad as I thought. Don't agree with some things though."

"Like what?"

They walked out of the church into the cool air. The trees lined the outside of the sanctuary. "I've already made some changes in my life. I didn't need to God to make those. You helped me make those."

She took a breath. "I'm not God. I can't make you keep those changes. I won't have all the answers when you need them."

"And God does?"

Hannah was about to answer when their mothers walked up to them. "You two ready to go?" Mrs. Evans asked.

They nodded and all of them drove home for Sunday dinner. Henry dropped Hannah and Mrs. Evans off at their house so they could rest, get changed for dinner and then he headed home. As usual, by four o' clock they came to the door. They feasted, maintaining light-hearted banter. Both Mrs. Evans and his mama said about five times how happy they were that he came to church this morning. He was beginning to rethink this, now they would want him to go every week. When they were done eating, he and Hannah helped wash up while their mothers relaxed on the porch. He was washing while she dried.

The light from the window was illuminating her face as she circled the cloth over the plate. "You know, I feel a bit nervous for you."

He washed the suds off the next plate. "Maybe I've banked too much on this. What happens if he doesn't give me the job?"

She put a dried plate in the cupboard and took the wet plate from his hands. "Then you'll find something else."

He started washing up the next plate. "Everyone will be disappointed."

"I'll still be proud of you," she said, smiling as she dried the plate.

"I gotta get this job so I can marry you."

Hannah faced him. "You're serious about this marriage thing, aren't you?"

Plunging his hand in the soapy water, he flicked some water at her. "You always think I'm joking, don't you?"

She dipped her hand in the water and flicked some water back at him. "That's because most of the time you are."

He cradled her face in his wet hands. "Do you think I'd be working so hard to get a job and so I can build you that house you want if I wasn't serious? Hannah, you haven't even let me touch you and I *still* want to marry you."

She feigned offense. "And you better remember that it's hands off until after 'I do'."

"So is that a yes?"

Gently, she removed his hands. "No," she said, wiping at her face. She went back to drying the dishes and he went back to washing. "Are you really gonna build that house?"

He turned back to the dishes, to hide his disappointment at her response. "Yes. Pale blue house with front and back porch, five bedrooms. Would you like to see my sketches?"

She smiled. "No."

He smiled. "I forgot you like surprises." He finished washing the last dish and handed it to her and then went to wiping down the table.

She walked over to the table and folded her arms. "If I agreed to marry you, then what?"

Copying her move, he sat down, arms folded over his chest. "You make it sound like a business deal."

Hannah pulled out a chair and sat down across from him. "I didn't mean it like that." She fidgeted on the seat. "Will you be faithful? Or are you just intrigued with me now because I've made this more difficult than the other girls?"

He placed his hands on the table. "I wouldn't want to marry you if I didn't intended on being faithful. I could go back to my old life."

She sighed and looked down, considering this. "You know Maureen hates me. Called me a dark skinned whore in front of the whole town and said I stole you away."

Henry's jaw tightened. "When was this?"

"That doesn't matter," she said, meeting his eyes. "I don't want to be discarded like she was and watch some other woman with you."

He closed his eyes. "I made a mistake. I will talk with Maureen and clear things up. But I promise things won't be like that with you."

"How can you promise me that?"

"You're just gonna have to trust me, Hannah."

Frustration seemed written on her forehead and she rubbed her eyes. "I don't know."

He put down his head. "Well, I'll give you the time you need to make up your mind."

She nodded and he got up. "I guess I'll go now."

She gave a weak smile and nodded. He left the house his chest feeling tight. Their mothers were still on the porch.

"Henry, where are you off to?" Miss Evans asked.

He turned around. "I just have something to take care of."

His mother looked at him, concerned. "Is everything alright?"

"Everything will be fine Mama. Thanks for the dinner Mrs. Evans. Mama, I'll see you later," he said as he left. He got into his car and drove off in the direction of Maureen's house. Her father was a lawyer and they owned a large white house with green shutters on the other side of town. After knocking on the door, their housekeeper, Olivia, answered.

"Henry," she said, looking surprised.

"Hi, Olive, I was wondering if Maureen was in."

"She is. Come in, I'll let her know you are here."

Henry stepped inside familiarizing himself the hunter green living room, with the rich mahogany furniture in the house, and the expensive rugs and vases that probably cost more than his mother made in a month. He took off his hat and sat down on one of the chairs Olive led him to.

"Her parents are away on business again, aren't they?"

"Yes."

He nodded. Her father was always away doing business, having affairs. Maureen's mother often traveled too, doing the same. This house was perpetually empty, the only real residents, Maureen and Olive. It had been one of the reasons he appreciated her, that she had the house to herself most times and he could come and go as he pleased. Maureen came down shortly, her light butter skin and hazel eyes radiant, but as he looked at her, he thought how much he wanted to see Hannah's dark, vivid eyes.

"Henry, what brings you here?" She said, her voice icy, not hiding one trace of her anger.

"Came to talk."

She sat in the leather chair across from him. "Decide to dump your whore and come back?"

"Maureen, that's enough. Hannah's no whore and you know it."

The set of her jaw was tight.

"I'm sorry, for the obvious pain I've caused you. I should've been honest with you a long time ago. I know we both agreed that it would be casual, but I knew you felt more than that and I never said anything."

Her eyes were watery. "So you really are in love with her?"

"I am."

"Well, she's made quite an achievement for herself. Made you surrender." She wiped at her eyes. "I still don't like her."

"I never expected you to. I wanted to make my own peace with you and hope you'll stop dragging her name through the streets."

Maureen licked her lips and then met his eyes. "I just don't understand Henry. You'd leave me for some darkie, who hasn't a cent to her name."

"You wanted to marry me and I haven't a cent to mine!"

"Yes, but you had goals and I could make Daddy give you some work once we married."

"I told you before, I wanted to earn it. Not have your Dad just write me a check."

"It still doesn't make any damn sense."

Henry leaned forward and looked her in the eye. "You know what makes no sense? The way you treat your fellow black woman. You think that it matters in the south, or to any white man, whether you're light or dark? You're still a Negro, Maureen. Ain't nobody letting you stay in their hotel or sit at a restaurant with you."

"I have ancestors from Spain and-"

"And no one gives a damn! All they care about is that you have some from Africa."

"Get out! I don't need this."

Henry clenched his jaw. "Maureen, I was hoping this would be an peaceful ending."

"Not when you choose that slut over me."

Henry put on his hat. "I hope you have a nice life," he said, walking to the door.

"I will...with Jeffrey."

He turned around. "Olsen? You'd sink so low to be with Olsen?"

She folded her arms. "I don't owe him anything unlike some people."

Henry opened the door himself. "If I know anything about him. He'll make your life hell. But, hey, if that's what you want, then you'll have money and your light skinned children." And with that he left.

By the time, he started to drive home it was already night, the stars bright against the black sky. That hadn't gone how he'd planned, but he'd known Maureen was a hard woman, and the fact that she was hurt by his actions didn't make matters better. Hearing that she was with Olsen was a recipe for disaster. He thought again about how conflicted Hannah seemed this afternoon. She loved him, but he couldn't think of any way to make her believe that he valued her more than all the other women he'd been with. He'd never agreed to build a house for a woman, told them his secrets, and waited more than a month before sleeping with them. But, none of those things phased Hannah. He began to think of how he could possibly propose to her, so she wouldn't doubt him. When he got to his house he went out back lying underneath the stars. Maybe if he bought her a really nice ring. But then again, he was sure Hannah was the type to want to pick out her own ring and money was the last thing to faze her. Exhaustion coupled with frustration made him rub his eyes and sit up. He looked out ahead at the mound of lilies a few feet ahead of him. He smiled and got up, racing in the house for shovels and then to Hannah's house. He grabbed the old ladder, checking to see its sturdiness.

He set it against the side of the wall and began to climb. When he got to Hannah's window, he tapped at it, not hearing anything. He tapped again and heard the opening of the window. Hannah popped her head out and looked at him against the side of the wall.

"What are you doing? You have a nightmare or something?"

"No, I need you to put on a pair of jeans and come with me."

"What?"

"Just do it, please."

"It's late. We have to be up in the morning. You have your meeting. I have work."

"I know, but this will be worth a little less sleep."

"I think you've lost your mind."

"Maybe I have."

She sighed. "Be careful on that thing... I'll be down in five minutes," she said, closing the window.

He went down the ladder with caution not wanting a repeat of nearly breaking his arm. He waited at the side of the house for her. She came down soon in an old shirt and jeans that showed the curve of her hips. Not many women wore them, but he was glad she'd bought one pair, she said, when she had stopped in New York City on her way back from Paris. Before he said something that would send her back in the house, he reached out to hand her a shovel.

"What in the world is that for?"

"For digging Hannah, I thought you were a smart girl."

She made a face. "I mean why would we be digging in the middle of the night?"

"Buried treasure, my dear. I heard there's some behind my house. I can get that money and use it to build that house for you," he said, trying to gage her reaction.

"You woke me up to dig for make believe gold?"

"Who said it's make believe?"

"Henry, I'm going back to bed, if you don't tell me the truth."

"Ok, ok, there's no treasure chest. But, I promise you, this will be worth it."

She snatched the shovel. "One hour. So, I suggest you dig fast."

He guided her to his backyard, to the mound of flowers. "Won't your mother kill us for ruining her garden?"

"She'll be fine. Trust me."

He put his shovel into the earth and began to pull up the flowers. Hannah followed suit. He dug furiously not wanting his hour to run out. As they dug, Hannah kept asking him if he was crazy and exactly why they were doing this. But, he'd only reached over and kissed her slowly and she'd remained quiet the rest of the time. He felt when his shovel hit something hard and he dug around it, pulling out the small wooden box. He brought it up out of the ground. His whole body was dirty, but he didn't care. He looked up at Hannah and saw her eyes widen with recognition.

"Was this worth your digging?" he asked her.

She didn't answer and he sat down on the ground exhausted and opened the box. She sat down next to him.

"The hearts from Mrs. Henderson's class," she said, pulling them out of the box.

He smiled as he watched her turn those hearts over in her hands. "I'm getting them all dirty," she said.

"They can be washed," he said, as he reached out for her hand. "Do you remember what I said when we buried these?"

She nodded.

"Marry me. I don't have fancy things to give you, but I will some day, even though I know you don't care about my money. But, I want to build you that house and give you a house full of children. You have always been the best thing I have and you always will be."

She looked down at the porcelain hearts. "I'll marry you on one condition."

He sighed. "What is it?"

"Promise me we'll stay in Idlewild. Marry here, raise our children here, even die here."

He rubbed circles with his thumb over her hand. "Yes, I didn't plan on ever leaving."

"Good," she said, smiling.

He leaned over and kissed her slowly. He rose up from her lips. "Thank God you said yes, it's only been three days and I was fresh out of creative ideas."

She chuckled and kissed him. "I couldn't watch you suffer any longer."

Resuming, he kissed her again until she was lying flat on the ground. She moaned softly. "And you say, that I'm trouble."

His hand roamed on the inside of her shirt and she smiled, "No funny business until after the wedding."

He settled his hand on her stomach. "None?"

She shook her head.

"Not even a little?"

"No," she said, kissing him.

He savored in the feel of her lips on his. "Then maybe we oughta quit kissing. I don't want your mama beating me with her skillet."

She laughed and then laid down on the dirt covered ground. "We're filthy."

"Yup. I could give you a bath, but you said no funny business."

She reached over and pinched him. "You definitely need a keeper."

"That's what you're for," he said, pulling her close. She laid her head against him and yawned. "Go to sleep."

"Out here?"

"Yes, ma'am."

She threw her arm around him and within minutes she was sound asleep.

Henry felt Hannah stirring against his chest and he saw her rise up. The sun was rising.

"Good morning," he said groggily.

She smiled. "Good morning."

He realized again how grimy they both were and he chuckled.

"If I were you, I wouldn't laugh. We need to get home before the generals catch us out here."

Both of them rose up. "You're right," he said, as he kissed her forehead. "We should get washed up, gotta go to Kingston's house."

They parted and Henry headed into the house and in the shower, careful not to waken his mother. He smiled contently in the shower, washing off all the dirt. He put on a pair of old trousers and headed downstairs making some breakfast. As he was scrambling some eggs, his mama came down stairs.

"Good morning," she said, sitting at the table.

"Mornin' Mama," he said, letting out a yawn.

"You know, you wouldn't be so tired if you didn't spend all night outside ruining my garden and sleeping on the ground."

Henry froze. He scooped the eggs into a plate and turned around. "Before you yell, I should probably tell you that I proposed to Hannah last night and she said yes."

She grinned. "You're still gonna plant back my flowers and no more all nighters with Hannah. I still got my values Henry."

"Yes ma'am," he said, grinning as he finished cooking and put the food in front of her. They ate in silence, both of them smiling every so often.

"I'm serious, Henry."

He finished his last bite, kissed her cheek, and threw her a wink before placing his dishes in the sink and heading upstairs to finish getting ready.

Henry knocked on Hannah's door, straightening his tie. She opened the door and he smiled at her through the mesh. She was wearing a burgundy ensemble today, with lipstick to match.

She stepped outside. "You look good. Very Handsome. I like your suit."

"I can't outdo you though."

The grin she gave him, made his heart beat intensely. "I told Mama this morning over breakfast."

"So did I."

He touched his forehead to hers for a few moments and breathed in her scent. "Let's go."

She walked over to the car and pulled the door open for herself. "I'm still the 20th century woman," she said, winking.

They drove in silence; just letting their hands hold on to each other. When they pulled up by the Kingston's summer home, he exhaled loudly.

"You'll be fine." She rested her hand on his arm. "Be yourself."

He took her hand, kissed it and then looked at the large taupe colored house surrounded by planted cypress trees. It had Spanish style architecture, not made from wood, but concrete with columns and a wavy tiled roof.

"This house is beautiful."

"Wait until you see inside."

They came to the front and the housekeeper answered and told him to wait in the living room for Dr. Kingston. Hannah was right. He thought Maureen had a nice house, but this one looked straight out of the pictures he'd seen of the European homes. There was cherry wood furniture, leather couches, expensive looking paintings and sculptures. Hannah gave him a smile and squeezed his hand softly before going off to her work with the children. Henry was nearly sweating when Dr. Kingston came in.

He was about the same height as Henry, but he was much thinner and sported glasses over his brown eyes. He had a firm shake, although his hand was veiny and leathery with age.

"Mr. Carrington. My office is this way." He led him down the hall filled with family photos, even paintings of them. His office had a large mahogany desk with dark brown leather chairs to match.

"Have a seat."

Henry sat and Dr. Kingston sat down in front of him and picked up Henry's sketch of the courthouse.

"I was very much impressed with your sketch, Mr. Carrington. Hannah tells me you're a fellow Howard University graduate," Dr. Kingston said.

"Yes, you graduated from there as well?"

"Yes, sir. Proud graduate." Dr. Kingston clasped his hands. "Now Mr. Carrington, we may as well cut to the chase, since I don't have much longer in Idlewild. I would like to hire you. You seem to be a good candidate and you come highly recommended by Miss Evans." He leaned back in his chair. "Although I'm assuming that she has a bias towards you."

Henry smiled lightly. "Yes, we just became engaged."

"I won't beat around the bush. I hear you have quite the reputation as a party boy and a drinker, I might add. I need someone I can rely on."

Henry felt a sinking feeling in his stomach. He closed his eyes for a few moments. He chose his words carefully. "I have no excuse for my behavior before. But, I can assure you that's not the case anymore."

"Explain."

"To be truthful, Hannah changed my life. Haven't had a drink in about two months. Felt terrible for the first couple of weeks, but I wanted to do it, to prove that I could. I'm not a squeaky clean person, and I can't promise you, I can't even promise Hannah that I'll never touch an ounce of booze again. But, I'm going to try as hard as I can, cause I don't want to disappoint her."

Dr. Kingston stroked his chin and exhaled. "Why do you want this job? Money? Status?"

"No, I want to build a house for her. Something she can call her own. Want to actually make something of my life. Make my mother proud and honor my father's memory."

"And what would you do if I gave the job to another?"

Henry swallowed. "I'd be disappointed, but I'd have to find something else. I'll do whatever I have to do to take care of Hannah and our mothers. Even if all three of them fight me because they know they can take care of themselves."

Dr. Kingston smiled. "Dealing with three independent women?"

For the first time in the meeting, Henry smiled. "Yes, sir. Been giving me fits all my life."

"Well, I know you love the women in your life. But, every man needs a little break from them." He handed Henry a few papers. Henry looked down at it. It was a train ticket to Atlanta, then one to New York, then Philadelphia, and Chicago, Detroit, then back to Idlewild.

"Sir?"

"We leave in a week. We gotta hit all those cities and get some funds from entrepreneurs, doctors, lawyers, you name it, if we want to build something of worth."

Henry smiled. "I don't know what to say."

"You don't have to say anything to me, but I suggest you go tell your lady," he said. He leaned in and whispered. "But, I'd bet that she's on the other side of that door listening."

Henry laughed. "Thank you so much, Dr. Kingston," he said, shaking his hand. Henry rose up and went to the door and sure enough Hannah was standing right there, her eyes wide with surprise that she'd been caught.

The rest of the week became a blur of packing and shopping for things to buy. He had to buy business suits, ties, cuff links, and shiny new black shoes. Pete insisted that a new watch was needed and spotted him some cash to buy it. Hannah had been disappointed that he'd be away for two months, but she couldn't stop smiling each time they went and he tried on one of those new suits.

It was now the night before he hopped on that train. He hadn't been back to the South and to be honest it made him a bit nervous. He had been lying awake for hours. He saw a light flicker and got up and looked out his window. Hannah was looking at him. She opened her window, smiled and then turned and went back inside her room.

Henry smiled and pulled on a shirt and some pants and made his way carefully downstairs and out into the cool September night. He walked to the side of Hannah's house and got the ladder and headed up. When he got in her room, she was laying down on the bed. Instead of taking the couch or the floor, he slipped in bed, spooning her.

"Nightmare?" she asked.

"No, just can't sleep."

"Neither can I."

The wind was blowing the curtains around softly. "I'll miss you."

She turned over to face him. "Yeah? How much?"

He chuckled. "Too much."

She kissed him. "Come back to me soon."

"Soon as I can," he said, running his hand over her hair.

She smiled mischievously. "I'm almost tempted to let you misbehave."

Henry felt his excitement surge. He burrowed his head against her neck, letting his lips brush against her skin. "Really?"

She sighed at the contact. "Maybe. I'm not sure."

He kissed her skin. She gasped and he asked. "Why?"

"You'll laugh."

He rose up and looked into her eyes. "Why would I laugh?"

"Cause I know nothing. I feel stupid."

He ran his thumb over her cheek. "Just tell me. I won't laugh."

She bit her lip. "I heard that it hurts."

"What hurts?"

"Sex."

He smiled and she pinched him. "You said you wouldn't laugh," she warned.

"Ok, ok." He sat up. "Maybe your first time, it'll hurt a bit, but after that I promise you'll like it. A lot."

She sat up now. "Why do you think I'll like it so much?"

He rolled his eyes and sighed. "Because of the sounds you make when I kiss you. You got some fire in you, Miss Hannah."

She smiled and he kissed her lips and trailed his kisses from her ear down to her jaw and then to her neck. "Yup, you gotta whole lot of fire. Might burn this house down," he said, and they both laughed softly.

His hands roamed over the sides her body and she touched his hands to stop him. "We have to stop."

Henry groaned. "You're probably right."

Her eyes were still wide, and she looked down. "I feel like a child."

He lifted her head. "You're not a child, you're just a virgin. It's kinda refreshing."

"Mama will hear us if we keep going," she said.

He put his hands behind him to settle himself. "That's fine. I wouldn't want your first time to be in your mother's house and having to be silent. Plus, I'm not too good at staying silent either."

She laughed quietly. "You're not disappointed?"

"I'm not." He pointed to his pants. "But he is."

She swatted at him. "What am I gonna do with you?"

"Marry me," he said, lying down on the bed. She laid down and fit herself against him again.

"I can't wait," she said softly.

"Me neither."

He had left Hannah's room shortly before the sun rose promising her to write and keep in touch. He had kept that promise. They corresponded as much as it would allow. With the Kingston's gone, Hannah had to find work and had offered to do Pete's books for some money, as well as continuing to help with the little girl's hair. He missed her and wished he could've brought her to Atlanta and to New York. He had been away for a month now, and already he knew they were half way there in collecting the needed funds for the hotel. It had been meeting after meeting, with a few short intervals in between to enjoy each city. He'd met wealthy black businessmen all over both Atlanta and New York and he was slated to leave tomorrow for Philadelphia. He entered his hotel room, looking at the bag of clothes on the chair he had bought for Hannah yesterday. She'd be excited when he wrote to her about it. He took off his shoes and tie and moved to the bathroom to get ready to shower before heading to bed.

There was a knock at the door and Henry groaned and headed to the door. He opened it and a bellhop was outside the door.

"Mr. Carrington?"

"Yes."

"Telegram for you."

He thanked the man and closed the door. He opened the telegram.

```
Urgent   STOP   House   fire   STOP   Mother,
Hannah, Mrs. Evans injured STOP Come Home END
                         Pete Charles
```

The Women are WILD

<u>Hannah</u>

Autumn had always been her favorite season in Idlewild. Hannah loved watching the trees turn from green to gold, to auburn, and eggplant. The trees looked like they'd been dipped in paint from afar, or that they'd been set ablaze. It was too cold to go in the lake, the stabbing needles claimed anyone who was brave enough to step in. But, she'd still come here and read in the afternoons, when it wasn't cold. She took out a pen and paper to write to Henry. Nothing much had happened though, since she'd last written him. She was still working for Pete and making a decent wage. Her mama and Mrs. Rosie had nearly finished her wedding gown, and even though she had doubted them, she had to admit that she loved it. Their mothers had obviously been saving up for this, and had ordered in silk fabric to make it. It had mutton sleeves that were in style, a train, and a strap for her to hold onto to keep it off the ground. The midriff and the sides of the dress were fitted to show off her figure. It had a sweetheart neckline and a draped bust. She couldn't believe they'd done all this for her; she was excited to put it on and see Henry's face.

Most of her days, she thought about him, hoping that he was keeping out of trouble and away from liquor. But, he'd been keeping his promise and she had to trust him, though the fear made her restless at night. She knew he'd probably be mad, but she'd been tucking away some money for a while to pay back Olsen. She'd brought back some money from Paris just in case she'd ever have to catch another train to find work. There was about $250 all together.

The only problem was getting Olsen not to open his big mouth. She put on her coat and gloves and headed out to town. She'd just slip by Olsen's to pay him, and then head to Pete's to help him out with the books, and do some cleaning. Henry had left his car for her to use and she was grateful. Hannah liked the long walks, but the frosty October air was making those walks not as pleasant as they once were.

When she reached town, she made sure to greet Mr. Cooper and then walked over to Olsen's office. He was running his practice out of one of the doghouses. She knocked the door, but didn't hear anything. She heard his voice inside, that low baritone. She wasn't going to leave and come back. Moving to the window, she groaned seeing the blinders closed. She let out a sigh of frustration and went to the next window, along the back of the building. Perhaps if he saw her face, he'd answer, probably thinking she'd taken him up on his offer. He was arrogant enough to think so.

She peered through the window. She saw Maureen and Jeffrey, his pants down and her skirt hiked up on the desk waiting for him. Hannah was so shocked by the sight that she nearly raced away from the office all the way to Pete's club. She took off her scarf and made her way to the table where she usually worked on the ledgers. He was sitting there smoking a cigarette and she asked him if he had an extra one. He handed her one, while looking at her strangely.

"Miss Hannah, you alright?"

Hannah looked at Pete's face, his forehead showing three lines across them. "Did you know about Maureen and Jeffrey?" she said, as she lit the cigarette.

He set down the glass in his hand and came and sat across from her. "Yes."

"Does Henry know?"

"Yes."

"I saw them today...they were on the desk."

He shook his head in confusion. "What?"

"They were on the desk," she stuttered.

"Doing what?"

"Having sex," she whispered.

Pete chuckled. "Oh." He fixed himself on his chair. "Well my dear, that's what men and women do."

Hannah cleared her throat and straightened her shirt. "I know. I just haven't seen anything like that up close. I mean I've seen pictures."

"Pictures?"

Her face felt hot. "At school. The girls had books with pictures."

He laughed heartily now, his hands on his large stomach. "And everyone thinks you girls are just there learning French, and how to become nurses and teachers."

Hannah smiled. "Henry probably wouldn't like me telling you that he hasn't had sex with me, would he? I mean, he would want to maintain his reputation."

"No. I don't think he's interested in keeping up his reputation in that way now that he has you."

Pete went behind the bar and tossed her the ledger. He picked up the glass he was cleaning and went back to working at the bar nearby. She was organizing through the profits Pete had made the night before. Following this ledger had been easy considering that Henry was so thorough. He had every income fully recorded for years and it was easy to see that Pete fully relied on the money from the summer to hold him throughout the year. In fact, Pete didn't make as much money as he did the summer before and he was gonna be short. Almost two hundred dollars short. Hannah reached into her pocket and felt the $250 dollars. There was no way Pete would take this money from her. She would have to find a way to anonymously give it to him. She put out the cigarette, finished up the ledgers, handed him the books, and grabbed her coat to head out.

"I have a question, Miss Hannah. How come your fiancée don't smoke?"

Hannah smiled slyly and then motioned him to come closer. "It'll make him wheeze. He has asthma."

Pete eyes glittered with glee and he laughed until he coughed. Hannah smiled, put a finger over her lips, and left.

Hannah closed the newspaper as her mother and Mrs. Rosie were sewing the lace trim on her veil. They had spent most of the evening building the fire to keep the place warm. If the present weather were any indicator, this winter would be fierce. Hannah smiled as she watched them making the veil. It seemed like the only thing they talked of nowadays was the wedding. She agreed with them that spring would be best. This winter was too cold to get married in. But, then according to the news marrying soon might be the best solution. She had left Europe to avoid the war and now it seemed like war was coming to America. Draft registration had begun and Henry would be a part of it. Hannah rubbed her forehead and set the paper aside.

"What's the news?" Mrs. Rosie asked.

"They're starting draft registration for the war."

Both women stopped sewing. Hannah's mama cleared her throat. "It's gonna be just fine. Henry will be fine," her mama said.

Hannah swallowed as she saw the way Mrs. Rosie's green eyes seemed frozen. "Yes, Mama's right Mrs. Rosie. Everything will be fine. Just keep it in prayer." She nodded and resumed sewing. Mrs. Rosie was fearless as far as Hannah knew, but the thought of losing her only son, would make any woman scared. Little did Henry know but when she was away at college she'd still write letters back home to her mother and then to Mrs. Rosie. It had been her idea for her to go away to Paris, to try something adventurous. It usually went that way, Mrs. Rosie pushed her to take a risk and Mama was there to give guidance and comfort along the way. She needed to talk with Henry. Hannah got some paper and began to write.

Henry,

I miss you very much and cannot wait for you to come home. We are all doing well, despite the cold weather. Don't worry my love; I have chopped enough wood to last us. A good deal has happened since I last wrote you. I have a confession to make. Two days ago I went to Jeffrey's office with the intent on paying him some of your debt. It was then that I discovered Jeffrey and Maureen in his office. I saw more than I feel comfortable writing. I left before they could see me. When I went to help Pete with his ledgers I noticed that he would fall short of some money. I gave the money to him anonymously because I know he'd never take the money from me. I will let you know if he mentions receiving anything when I see him later this week. Henry, I've been reading the news and it has been making me nervous. Scared even... I just don't know what our future would hold if the war interrupted our lives. I suppose I will just have to take my fears to God in prayer. I hope you are collecting thousands. I look forward to seeing the new hotel. Perhaps we can have dinner there someday. Please hurry home, so I can smell the cinnamon on your mouth from the candy you eat to curb your cravings for alcohol. I never realized how much I wanted that. Or how your body is always warm. Warmth would be good now in this weather. I suppose I am being very scandalous...I'm sure you will like this letter and follow it up with your own scandalous thoughts and wishes.

Yours,

Hannah

Hannah put the letter into an envelope and sealed it. She put it into the pocket of her apron and went back to the room where her mama and Mrs. Rosie were working.

A few days later she received back a scandalous letter. She could hardly wait to open it when she got it from the post office in town. She read it over and over the whole way going to Pete's office. Grinning the whole way, she swore others could just tell the things he had written from the look on her face.

What have I done to the sweet, innocent Hannah? I share the same longing to feel my hands on your waist, to smell the vanilla on your skin. I'm afraid if I touch you again, I will not keep my promise to leave you a virgin so I suppose I should try and quiet these thoughts. Just remember though that you started it.

The money is coming along Hannah. We have risen a good deal for the short amount of time. I won't discuss you going to give money to Olsen, I'm sure you already know my thoughts on that. I am thankful that circumstances prevented you giving the money to Olsen. Although, I know that Pete would never take it from you, but he deserves that money. I hope you took some to help take care of things in both our houses.

As for the draft, please do not worry yourself. I do not plan in fighting in an army that does not respect Negroes, and leaving my wife and mother to fret for my life.... My dear,

I must go now. I love you and I look forward to your next letter and even more, the day I return home to you.

Yours,

Henry

Hannah made her way to Pete's, tucking the letter into the pocket of her coat. Pete was wiping down the counter and the smell of Johnson's Glo-Coat was heavy in the atmosphere. She sat at the bar as he said his greetings to her. He had told her two days ago that he had gotten the money and she'd written it into the ledger. He was so happy, said that maybe God does answer prayer.

"Why do you have that smile on your face? Get a letter from your man?"

She smirked. "Yes. Can I have some water please?"

Pete got her the water and then lit a cigarette. "You been a smoker for a while, Miss Hannah? You smoked the other day like you've done it before."

"Yes, I have a few times. I liked it and it became a nasty habit. But, it gives me foul breath so I don't usually do it."

Pete chuckled. "Who would've thought that you'd like smokes?"

"I'm not always as innocent as I appear."

"No?"

"No one is."

"True. Everyone has vices. What's yours?"

Hannah smiled and sipped some of the water. "Well for one, there's the smoking. I can lose my temper quite easily. Henry knows that. The rest, I'll keep to myself," she grabbed some peanuts from his dish. "Your turn to spill."

He exhaled some of the smoke and watched the smoke curl and dance and then fade up into the air. "Well, the smoking and I have a jealous streak."

"Jealousy?" Hannah said, raising an eyebrow.

"Yes, I'm happy for you, truly I am. But, sometimes even this old man is jealous of you and Henry. I was a lot like Henry when I was younger. Used to drink a whole lot. Got real mean when I drank. I'd yell at my wife and even knocked her around a few times. Then one morning I woke up and she was gone. I never saw her again. Sometimes I wish I could've found the strength to give up the bottle like your man."

"So why do you sell it then?"

"I was doing this when I met my wife. It's the only thing I'm good at, and I'll probably never make this much money with something else."

"If another opportunity came your way, would you leave all of this?"

"Honestly? No, I couldn't leave it for her. I don't think I ever will."

"So why'd you give up the drinking then?"

"I did that for me. Got tired of waking up in a fog, vomiting at nights, and being in bad situations."

Hannah nodded and thought back to the night she'd seen Henry bloodied by the man outside the club. "Did you ever try to find her? Your wife?"

He smiled softly. "No, I figured I'd given her enough hell and I'd let her live her life. She probably has those children she always wanted now."

"Did you want kids?"

He grabbed some of the peanuts and started to munch on them. "I did want a boy. Someone to teach some things to, guess Henry kinda became that for me."

Hannah smiled. "I want girls. Is that bad that I think I only want girls?"

"Nah, everyone has a preference even if they lie and say it doesn't matter."

They both laughed. "If you had a boy, what would you have named him?" Hannah asked.

"Oh, I don't know...my wife and I always said we would've named him Benjamin. We liked that name."

Hannah rolled the name around in her head. "I like it too."

Pete put out the cigarette and threw the rest of peanuts in his mouth. "Enough about this, my dear. It brings back memories I should forget." Pete grabbed a broom and began to sweep the floors. Hannah looked at the clean and shiny wood floors. The memories had him flustered.

"I can do it, Pete. You pay me for it."

He held up his hand. "It's alright. Go home, and don't you worry yourself about me Hannah." He slipped her a cigarette and winked at her. "Let your hair down before your man comes home."

Hannah kissed his cheek. "Thank you Pete, for everything." He nodded and she put on her coat and headed outside to the car.

Although the cold bit into her skin and touched her bones, Michigan was still beautiful during this time and alive with color from the trees. She went to the market to pick up some of the cherries they all liked so much. She'd barely made it outside before she put one of the deep red, sweet cherries in her mouth. Maureen was standing outside the marketplace, her brown hair curled to perfection with her hat. She stared her down with those hazel eyes.

"Hello. Is something wrong?"

"Nothing," Maureen said shrugging. "Just still puzzled over what Henry sees in someone like you."

Hannah spit the cherry pit on the ground near Maureen's feet. "Like me?"

"That's right."

"It's funny, usually women who have sex with men they're not married to on their office desks, are called sluts."

Maureen went still.

She continued. "Although she may deserve it, I would never go as far to shame a woman like that in public."

"Why wouldn't you?" Maureen whispered.

"Because I figure that she may be just nursing a broken heart, so she's been making some hasty and terrible decisions."

Maureen cleared her throat and Hannah could see her eyes becoming glassy.

"You know, you could do a lot better than a corrupt lawyer."

Maureen rolled her eyes. "Yes, I bet this is where you tell me I could've gone to college like you."

"No, this is where I tell you that I used to wish I looked like you. I wanted to be just as tall and have your skin and eyes. You can have any man you want."

Maureen looked down at her. "I can't have Henry though."

Hannah really did feel bad for her and she smiled softly. "No, you can't have Henry."

"There are no good men in Idlewild. They're too lazy."

Hannah laughed now and Maureen even smiled. "Yes, as they say, the men are idle and the women are wild." She dug in her bag and pulled out a cherry. "Here," she said handing one to Maureen. "They always cheer me up."

Maureen took one and popped it in her mouth.

"You can leave Idlewild. Go to another city, meet a man, fall in love again…"

"I always liked Chicago."

Hannah dug in the bag and tossed her another cherry. "Chicago, it is then."

Maureen smiled and Hannah turned to leave. "Thank you."

"Yeah, yeah," Hannah said. "Just don't let Olsen sleep with you anymore."

Maureen smirked, "I still don't like you, Hannah. But, at least you're not as dumb as I thought," she said, and turned into the market. Hannah got into the car and drove home. She'd always loved the pathway to her house, the trees on both sides of the driveway. When she got home she called out to her mama that she'd gotten some cherries and they settled at the table across from each other. There was one bowl that Hannah put the cherries in and another for the pits. Hannah ran her hand over the blue gingham tablecloth and reached into the bowl for a cherry.

"Mama. I need you to tell me everything I need to know about marriage."

Her mama laughed. "There's a lot to tell missy."

"Well start from the beginning. What should I know about...the wedding night?"

Hannah's mother pulled a pit out her mouth and placed it in the bowl. She wiped her hands on her apron. "What do you want to know?"

"I'm not sure," Hannah said nervously. "What should I expect?"

Her mother took a breath. "Nothing bad Hannah. It will be wonderful...it's hard to explain."

Hannah nodded and pulled a pit out of her mouth. "I asked Henry if it will hurt. He said maybe my first time and then after no."

Her mother smiled softly. "Been talking to Henry about that?" she chuckled. "He's right, and with someone as *experienced* as Henry, I'm sure he'll know what he's doing."

Hannah put the pit in the bowl and laughed. "Oh lord, Mama!"

"Don't mama me. And don't think I don't hear you two at nights. Even the night before he left."

Hannah froze. Her mama smiled and continued, "I was young once. But, don't let it happen again. I don't think Henry wants me chasing him out this house."

The pile of cherry pits in the bowl was rising.

"Mama, so what does it feel like to have a baby?"

She raised an eyebrow the way Hannah always did, and she could see herself in her Mama's face. The same brown eyes, small pout, and dark hair that grew lighter at the tips. Mama leaned forward, her breasts pressing against the table. "Does it look pleasant?"

"No, not that part. I mean what does it feel like to have the baby grow inside you?"

"Oh, well I suppose it's different for every woman. Some get sick, some can't stop eating everything in sight, and some are as cool as a cucumber."

"I hope I have babies."

"You will."

Hannah sighed. "What should I do when Henry and I fight?"

"Stand your ground," her mama said sharply. Then she flashed her hand. "Unless you're wrong, but we women are never wrong."

They both laughed at that and Hannah looked outside at the sun going down. Mrs. Rosie was still next-door and it would be a cold night. Hannah's house had a better fireplace.

"I think I should go get Mrs. Rosie. It's going to be a cold night."

Her mother gathered the bowl of pits and moved to the trash bin. "Yes, go get her. She'll be there pretending she's fine. Tell her we're not taking no for an answer. Henry isn't home to make sure the fire in the house keeps her warm."

Hannah grabbed her coat and headed outside. Her face felt like it was being sliced by each cold wind that blew her way. When she finally made it to the Carrington's door she banged hard so that Mrs. Rosie would hear her. Mrs. Rosie pulled the shade on the window close by the door and looked at her before moving to the door and opening it.

"Hannah? What are you doing out here in this cold girl?" Her hair that was always the color of wet sand was plaited down her back.

Hannah stepped in the house and Mrs. Rosie closed the door behind her. "I came to get you. It's cold in this house. Have you built a fire?"

"Child, I can last the night without the fire."

"Mrs. Rosie, we know you're afraid of building your own fire. Come over to my house I already have a fire going."

"No, it's alright."

"Mama said that I'm not supposed to take no for an answer."

"Your mother is a stubborn woman."

Hannah smiled. "Not as stubborn as the woman insisting she stay in a cold house."

Mrs. Rosie laughed. "Yes, I am the queen."

"Come on, queenie, let's get you to some warmth." Hannah said, pulling her hand gently. "No queen should sleep in the cold."

"Ok, ok, let me get my things," she said, moving to the stairs.

She went up the creaking stairs and Hannah called out for her to hurry. Hannah kept moving in the house to keep the heat in her body. She looked around and smiled at the tacky red plush chair and the battered yellow couch against the bland décor of the house. Mrs. Rosie didn't care for the home décor as much as for making some good meals and sewing dresses. Hannah had always found it odd that the woman who could sew almost anything hadn't sewn herself some better curtains or bedding. She was sure that Henry would let her design their house anyway she wanted, and she hoped they wouldn't fight over it too much.

Mrs. Rosie came down the stairs with her bag and coat in hand. She stuck her feet in her boots, and they left the house into the tundra that made them almost convulse when the wind hit them. Hannah tried to move as fast as she could in the cold, but she had to keep stopping to make sure she wasn't leaving Mrs. Rosie behind. But, Lord knows she wanted to just sprint right into the warmth of her house. When they got into the house both of them breathed a sigh of relief. Hannah went straight to the fire to warm her hands a bit. They were stiff and she tried bending her fingers. Mrs. Rosie did the same.

"Thanks for coming for me," Mrs. Rosie said, "Sometimes being stubborn as a mule isn't a good thing."

Hannah smiled and kissed her cheek. "There's a cold kiss just for you."

Mrs. Rosie laughed and went back to warming herself. Hannah's mama came downstairs. "Oh, so you got her to come. Lord knows if it were me it would've taken a hour."

Mrs. Rosie waved her hand dismissing her playfully. "Because I love my daughter in law more than you, Mae."

Hannah's mama pinched Mrs. Rosie before taking a seat on the couch. "Oh, you watch how they'll both leave us once they get married."

Hannah smiled slyly at her mother. "You love to start trouble mama."

"No, just speaking the truth."

Mrs. Rosie sat on the couch next to Hannah's mama. "Yes, Mae, we'll be all alone. That is, until they start having babies and then they'll need us."

Hannah smiled. "Of course. And I'll need you two whenever Henry gets me angry enough to make me scream."

"That'll be nearly everyday," Mrs. Rosie said.

"Good, so then you know I won't stop needing you."

Mrs. Rosie sighed. "Yes, I think Mae and I agree that we want to be of help to you both until we can't be here no more."

"I'm sorry. I don't understand. I thought the two strongest women would live forever," Hannah said, folding her arms.

"When I was young like you, I thought so too. But now I know that's impossible."

"You two aren't *that* old."

Hannah's mama laughed. "Yes, Rose, we should take that as a compliment."

Both of the women laughed heartily and Hannah could see the laugh lines around their mouths and their eyes. She hoped that one day she'd have those same laugh lines as evidence that she'd lived a full life.

They sat there for the next two hours talking about everything from the church, to the wedding, to Henry's return back home. As much as each of them would complain about his antics, they all missed him and Hannah suspected that Mrs. Rosie missed him the most.

"Ahh, well, I'm off to bed," Hannah's mama said, rising from the couch.

"Me too," Mrs. Rosie said.

"Mrs. Rosie, just take my room. I'll just sleep here close to the fire."

"You sure?"

"Yes ma'am."

They said their goodnights and Hannah relaxed on the sofa and read for a bit. After reading three chapters of *Their Eyes Were Watching God*, she laid her arm across her forehead and lay there just thinking of how much longer it would be until Henry would be home. She turned her head to the left in direction of the fireplace and the white of the cigarette in the pocket of her coat caught her eye. Smiling, she thought of Pete telling her to let her hair down, she took the pins out her hair, and lay back against the couch letting her hair fall against the arm of it. Turning the cigarette over in her fingers, she thought back to the last time she had smoked one of these had been with the gardener back in Paris. After they had finished dancing for the day, he pulled out a cigarette and muttered in French that he needed a smoke after a long day. The gardener handed her one and she lit it, closed her mouth, and let the smoke seep out through her nose like some kind of dragon.

Henry would probably never believe that she had liked the feeling of the smoke filling her lungs. She thought it made her look quite sexy too. Moving close to the fireplace, her hand carefully let the embers of the fire light the cigarette. She took a draw on it and hoped that no one would smell the smoke. It had been an hour since they'd gone to bed. Savoring the smoky flavor for a while, Hannah got off the couch and went to the stove to make some tea, cigarette still in hand. She turned on the gas when she heard a sound at the window. Walking over revealed that it was just the wind blowing one of the chairs on the porch. It would have to wait until morning. Hannah went back to the kitchen and put the cigarette in her mouth and struck the match for the stove. Too much smoke entered her mouth and she coughed and dropped the match on the stove. A loud booming sound rang in her ears and she felt the sharp pain as her head hit the wall. There was the smell of burning hair and she reached behind her to touch her head, but her hands stung. She felt disoriented as she tried to stand and put out the fire that was now raging against the stove.

Hannah reached for something to throw to put out the fire when she turned and saw that the embers from the stove had lit the blue gingham tablecloth on fire. Trying to rise up again, the pain radiated through her palms. She looked down now her singed hands, red and raw. Forcing herself to the kitchen counter, again Hannah attempted to grab a bowl, but her hands wouldn't allow her. She dropped the bowl, and it fell spreading porcelain chips everywhere. It was then she heard her mother's voice calling for her, but the world was still spinning a bit, and the fire was dancing on the table, the stove, and all those flames began to blend. They looked like the trees in the fall, and the smoky smell was strong, like she had smoked fifteen cigarettes at once. Guilt washed over her as she continued hearing her mom call out for her, and then she heard screaming. The screams she'd imagined every time they talked about that place of weeping, wailing and gnashing of teeth in church. Screams of terror and then the screams of pain.

Hannah woke to the pungent smells of vinegar. She raised her hand to cover her nose and felt the scratchiness of the gauze that covered her hands like mittens. She opened her mouth to scream, but the dryness in her throat overpowered her. Pete rushed to her bedside, shushing her.

"Miss Hannah, relax!"

Hannah rested against the bed, and looked around at the blue walls, with the mismatched curtains, and the old wood furniture. She was in Henry's room. It was then she remembered the loud boom of the gas stove, and the pain that radiated in her head afterward. The pain began to swell as she rose up, looking around wildly. Henry came in then with a glass of water, his white shirtsleeves rolled up.

"You're up," he said, with a faint smile.

Hannah moved to speak again, but couldn't, and he moved towards her with the water. She wanted to take it from him and drink by herself, but the gauze was strangling her hands. He told her to open her mouth, and began to pour the water gently, but the water was so cold against her hot, dry throat that she spit up on him like an infant. He chuckled a bit, tried again, and she took the water better this time, wetting her throat enough to speak.

"It smells."

He put the glass on his drawer, and touched her gauze covered hands. "Sorry, it's the vinegar and chamomile the doctor said to keep on your hands so they heal."

"How bad are they?"

"Second degree burns. The doctor said you should look fine after they heal completely. Maybe some scars after."

Hannah closed her eyes and rested back on the bed. But, as soon as she did the sounds of the screams came back to her. The piercing screams. She remembered being dragged out before she went back into the pit of darkness.

"Where are Mama and Mrs. Rosie?"

Henry touched her arm softly, the same touch Mr. Rousseau had given her when they told her Claire had passed on. Her eyes flew to his and he choked on his words before he said them properly. "They burned too bad Hannah. They didn't make it."

Hannah shook. Shook so much that Henry had to hold her and Pete closed his eyes as she shook and wailed. Was this the weeping, wailing and gnashing of teeth that was written in red letters in the Bible? She kept on like that until she felt light headed. Until she felt like she was floating again. Until she grew limp in Henry's arms and didn't make another sound until morning again.

Some glad morning when this life is over
I'll fly away
To a home on God's celestial shore
I'll fly away

Henry nodded to well-wishers while Hannah stood still staring ahead under her black hat that Henry had bought for her two days ago. Some of her hair had gone in the fire and it had to be cut. She'd cut it off herself in the bathroom, much to Henry's horror when he came in and saw all the hair in the sink. The hat covered her hairline and eyebrows that were growing back, and made her look in a perpetual state of surprise. The choir was sure singing that song. She remembered that Mama had always liked that song. That song and Victory in Jesus. She fought the burning in her eyes from the unreleased tears as the choir continued on.

I'll fly away, Oh Glory
I'll fly away, in the morning
When I die, Hallelujah bye and bye
I'll fly away, I'll fly away

Mrs. Rosie loved that chorus. Especially when the men came in on those end parts, their bass voices anchoring the choir. Yes, she supposed that both Mama and Mrs. Rosie must be in heaven somewhere rejoicing with the angelic choir. It had been a week and Hannah's hands had come out of their binding now, and she was able to wipe at her face, as the tears streamed down.

There was still a bandage on her left leg, close by her calf where the skin was charred and resembled tree bark. The smell of aloe vera remained on her hands, and despite the tingling pain, she let the salty tears drop on them.

She deserved every sting that racked her body. She could've put that fire out. She should've put that fire out, instead of her mama having to brave the flames, drag her out, and then go back for the terrified Mrs. Rosie. That's what Henry told her. Mama had gone back in for her best friend and both of them had gotten trapped in the fire, as she lay outside unconscious in the cold Michigan air, while they burned. Hannah was mad at Henry for not blaming her, even when she told him that if she hadn't been balancing that cigarette in her mouth, she could've lit the stove better, and that none of this would've happened. No, he only just shushed her and told her to stop blaming herself, like someone would tell a child, who'd lost their mother. But, every day those heavy dark circles were still under his eyes. He couldn't sleep at night because he knew that she was to blame and he couldn't just tell her to her face.

Henry touched her hand lightly now, she squeezed back to assure him she was fine, and to feel that slight tinge of pain radiate through her palm. Hannah didn't even know why they bothered with the casket. There were barely any of their bodies left once the fire department on Lake Drive came, and put out the flames and carried Hannah off to the hospital. Henry and the church members had given them the funeral they could afford and deserved. Even though the flowers were out of bloom, they had managed to still make a wreath of some wildflowers to bury each of them with. Later, they all walked to the graveside, singing loudly,

Victory in Jesus

My Savior forever!

He sought me and he bought me

With his redeeming blood

He loved me ere I knew him

And all my love is due Him

He plunged me into victory beneath the cleansing flood.

They sang it even as the deacons put the coffins in the ground side by side, and Rev. Washington began to say, "We therefore commit Mae Evans and Rose Carrington's bodies to the ground; earth to earth, ashes to ashes, dust to dust; in the sure and certain hope of the Resurrection to eternal life." Hannah sang it until her voice broke and she couldn't utter another word. But, she could still hear Henry singing alongside her as they shoveled the dirt on top. He never stopped singing until every soul from that graveside left them and they were completely alone.

Hannah woke to the light shining on her face from the window. She got up and looked in the mirror, the crust prominent around her eyes, like someone who'd let fresh snow fall on them. She went to the bathroom and splashed the water across her face. Her eyebrows were now back to their thick shape, her hands were able to flex and press on the sink without pain. A month had gone by slowly. She had settled in her routine of staying in the house and avoiding the outside. Henry would leave each day rounding up workers for the buildings and still doing Pete's ledgers. When he came home in the nights he would come in the bed and curl against her, asking her how her day went. It was always the same answer. She had done nothing except read and clean. She cleaned when there was nothing to clean, and the rest of the time she just sat there in the house. Only on Sundays, did Henry drag her out the house to church. If she wasn't in such a fog she might laugh that she was actually being forced to go to church by Henry of all people.

But, Hannah had to admit that it did help somewhat to hear the choir sing and see the smiles on their faces as Rev. Washington screamed on about crossing over Jordan and told them to say AMEN. Hannah now brushed her teeth and heard the sounds of frying. She moved downstairs cautiously. Usually Henry was gone and had left breakfast out for her by now. When she got downstairs he was standing by the stove scrambling eggs.

"No work today?" she asked, folding her arms and leaning against the wall.

"No, you and I are going out to town today."

"For what?"

"Gotta find you something to wear for the wedding."

"What wedding?"

"Ours. You can't avoid the gossips with us just living here together."

"We haven't even..." Hannah said, as Henry slipped the eggs out the frying pan and on to a plate. "Besides I thought you didn't care about the gossips."

"I don't. But, you do. You will, once you get out this fog."

Hannah sat down at the kitchen table. "I don't want to get married without them."

"Neither do I. But, we gotta move on somehow. You can't spend all your days in here, fading away. Look at you, you're skin and bones." She looked into his eyes that were the green that encircled a flower before it bloomed. The dark circles under the eyes only intensified the green there. He sat down in front of her and pushed the plate of eggs towards her.

Hannah took a deep breath. "And you just ignoring everything and working like a mule is helping, huh?"

He rubbed his tired eyes. "No, it ain't helping me. That's why I want us to get married and at least try and move past this."

Hannah laughed sarcastically and then he lost it. Really lost it.

"You think I'm happy living in this house with all these memories!"

Hannah sat frozen, watching him rub his hand through his brown hair. "I loved them too!" he screamed, his spit falling onto the eggs and his fist pounding the table so hard she thought it might flip over. "And I'm trying like hell to keep you satisfied! To lie in the bed with you every night and not shed a tear! To go out and work and put some food on the table and not spend it on booze! I do that for you! I do that for them!"

He went to that old, yellow, beaten up sofa and just laid there. He was silent and Hannah couldn't tell if he was crying, or on the verge of another fit. She picked up the plate of eggs and walked towards him slowly. She sat on the little space available since his big body was sprawled out. She leaned down and kissed his eyes finally tasting the salt there.

She cut a piece of the eggs with her fork and pushed it into her mouth. "I'll be good. I promise."

He just kept crying until she had eaten almost all those eggs and then the last bite left on the plate she pushed into his mouth. He chewed slowly watching her. She fit her small body on top of his. "See? I'm being good now." He smiled and they just lay there for a while until they fell asleep, like two children exhausted after a tantrum.

The wedding was in the church a week later. Hannah had bought a simple dress from a store in Grand Rapids, and had pinned her hair up and tucked some of the flowers that looked like babies breath to disguise the uneven ends of her hair. She invited everyone they knew out to the church, including all the little girls whose hair she used to do, and their fathers, Robert, and even all the construction workers. Henry had thought she would want to keep it small, but no she wanted it so big that there was no room left in the church. That way she wouldn't have to see the empty seat where her mama and Mrs. Rosie were supposed to be sitting. There weren't as many people in Idlewild now that it was late October, but with everyone gathered together in Tabernacle AME, it was warm despite the autumn chill outside. The reception at

Pete's kept some of the church members away, those who wouldn't be caught in a house of liquor. The people of Idlewild never failed to surprise. They took care of everything, the cake and food. They brought enough food to last them a whole month. They handed Henry bath salts, bubble baths for his new wife and Hannah got silk, lace and sheer gowns. Hannah was so giddy that she even took a drink of some wine herself and fed Henry some too. While the men sat back drinking, the women took to the dance floor and eventually got the men on their feet. The place was alive with the hoots, hollers, and laughs of the townspeople, as they kept moving to stay warm inside the club. Henry had rubbed his hand across her bottom softly and his eyes sparkled with mischief. When they tumbled back into the house later they were both laughing like teenagers who'd just pranked neighbors.

Hannah ran up the stairs as Henry moved to the fireplace and put some fresh logs in. She went to the bathroom and went under the water. It was cold and she could only afford herself a few minutes before she would be shaking like she had epilepsy. She cleaned under her arms; she cleaned the rest of herself like her mama had told her about the day they had sat there eating those cherries. When she came out she wrapped herself in a towel and opened the door to find Henry standing there.

He looked at her for the longest time; she could hear the crackling of the wood in the fire, and the songs that the crickets sang at nights.

"Stay like that while I wash off myself."

Hannah looked at him confused. "You don't want me to put

on something? Maybe one of the gowns I got as a present?"

"Not tonight. Just stay like that in the towel."

He moved into the bathroom. "You can go downstairs by the fire while I wash."

She felt awkward to tell him now that she was afraid to be in front of that fire all by herself. That the sounds of the fire popping the wood, would only remind her of the wood cracking all around her as the fire tore through her house. That's why she had moved Mrs. Rosie's bed so that she didn't have to face the direction of the empty land that was once her house. Henry might think it was strange, but she liked sleeping on Mrs. Rosie's bed when Henry had left for work in the morning, and smelling her familiar scent, the rose scented bath soap she had. If she didn't have anything to keep from her own mama, then she would fill herself of the woman who had been a second mother to her. The woman that would've been her mother-in-law. She heard the pipe going and she sat there on the floor, goosebumps covering her, and she pulled her knees and the towel closer to her chest.

Hannah tried to remember her mother's words that Henry would know what he was doing and there was nothing to worry about. She could taste the cherries once more and she leaned her head back against the wall. Her body was still shaking, partly from the cold and partly from her nerves. Hannah sighed loudly and then laughed at herself for being nervous. The pipes turned off and she stood up, waiting for him to open. When he did, he had a towel tied around his waist. Hannah imagined that maybe the Egyptians had looked that way in their glory. If she believed in reincarnation she might dare say that Henry was Moses himself.

"How come you didn't go downstairs?" Henry said, gently.

Hannah only shrugged and rose up on her toes to kiss him softly.

He smiled softly and kissed her once again trailing his kisses to her jaw and down her neck. "I was planning on going slow tonight," Henry said.

"Then don't."

Henry chuckled, his laugh vibrating on her neck. "You're a virgin. Going too fast won't be a good thing."

"Oh."

Henry picked her up in one swoop and then took her to his bedroom. "I thought we were going by the fire?" Hannah asked.

"Changed my mind," Henry said, as he placed her on the bed and the towel she had been holding tightly to herself became undone. He lit a lamp and Hannah lay there confused. Didn't people couple together in the dark?

Hannah watched him remove his towel and stared at him before averting her eyes. He laughed softly and leaned down on the bed to kiss her. "It's ok to look, we're married now."

Hannah couldn't find the words to say as his hands roamed across her body. She almost reached for him to stop before she felt the sensations course through her. She pulled her arms back to the pillow on her right and the edge of the bed on her left for support. Then suddenly she thought she would wet herself right on this bed in front of Henry. But, before she could pull away a shuddering began in her body. Henry raised up, smiling.

When she was done shuddering she whispered, "Was that supposed to happen?"

"Yes."

"That's normal?" She asked again.

"You tell me, did it feel good?"

Hannah nodded and Henry leaned in to kiss her again. "I thought I was having a fit."

Henry laughed hard now, his golden chest heaving up and down as he lay beside her. She wanted to slap him, but as she saw his face creased with laughter, she began to chuckle too. He leaned in again to kiss her face and then kissed his way down her body, he spent extra long at the places the skin was healing from the burns.

"Am I supposed to be doing something? Something for you?"

He smiled. "You're doing fine. Tonight will be for you."

"The rest might hurt, but just this once."

Hannah nodded nervously.

Henry hesitated and Hannah smiled shyly up at him. "It's ok. You're my husband now. I don't have anything to be afraid of."

Hannah rose up and laid herself across his chest. "I liked that," she said, playing with the fine hair across his upper chest.

"You did?"

"Yes, you said that now it won't hurt so bad anymore."

"No, it shouldn't. But we'll still take it slow for a few more times," he said, rubbing his hand on her hair.

"Can we stay in this house?"

He stiffened. "Why? Don't you want your dream home?"

"Things were different then. I want this house. I want to keep the furniture, everything."

"Hannah..." he said, sitting up.

"Please? If I decorate it a bit, will you let us stay? You can build onto it."

"What about your claw foot tub, and five bedrooms for your kids?"

"We can still buy the tub."

He held her hand and brought it to his lips. "Remember what we said about moving on? I won't tear down the house or nothing, but I can't stay here with all of mama's things."

Hannah nodded. Henry kissed her hands again, "We start building in the spring. You'll love the new house. I promise."

She nodded again and he rose up from the bed. "I'm gonna put out the fire downstairs."

Henry left the room and after a while he came back. When he did, Hannah feigned sleep, she heard him turn off the lamp, and then settle in bed next to her again.

He rubbed her head. "It will be fine, you'll see," he whispered.

The next morning Hannah awoke, her body sprawled over his golden one. She stretched herself like a feline and Henry awoke. She looked at him awhile, even though there were yellow flecks of crust around his eyes.

She chuckled and burrowed her face in the pillow. "You look a mess."

"And your breath smells," he said, as he pinched her lightly.

She rose from the bed taking the sheet with her to cover herself. Henry tugged the sheet from her. "Greedy man," Hannah said, as she went to the drawer and pulled out a shirt to cover herself with. The shirtsleeves flopped over her arms, and the hem of the shirt brushed her knees.

"What do you want for breakfast?"

He turned over to look at her, balancing his head on his fist, "You're going to cook?"

"Yes."

"You sure?"

"I'm sure Henry," she said, as she continued to button up the shirt.

He looked at her for a while, "Flapjacks and eggs."

"Bacon, too?"

"If you can manage it."

She rolled up the sleeves of the shirt as tight as she could around her arms. "If you remember correctly, I cook better than you."

Henry rolled his eyes and turned over. "Prove it."

Hannah smiled, went to brush her teeth, and then go downstairs. She prepared the batter for flapjacks as she heard Henry start showering. Rubbing a bit of margarine on the pan, as she removed her hand from the handle of the pan, she saw the mark of sweat there. Moisture filled her under arms. She swallowed hard as she turned on the gas and then lit the match. Letting out a small yelp, she lit the stove and watched the flame envelope the bottom of the pan. She exhaled deeply and then poured the batter on the pan. The small sizzling, cracking, and popping sound mixed with the sound in her memory of the wood snapping, and she felt her heart rate increased. The thrumming of her blood reverberated through her whole body and she turned over the flapjack mechanically.

"Smells good," Henry said, and she turned to see him coming down the stairs. She removed the flapjack from the pan and put it on a plate, as he came behind her. He nuzzled his face in her neck and her body stiffened. He would distract her and she would burn the place.

"What's wrong?"

"Can you finish the breakfast for me while I take a shower?"

When she turned around, she only met his eyes for a moment before dropping them back to the floor.

"Sure."

She walked off, heading to the stairs, feeling ashamed.

"Hannah."

She turned around as Henry was pouring some more batter onto the pan. "It's ok, one step at a time. 20th century women get scared too. Give yourself time."

She nodded and went upstairs.

Jesus knows all about our struggles;
  He will guide 'til the day is done:
There's not a Friend like the lowly Jesus:
  No, not one! No, not one!

Hannah sung softly as they closed the service with the hymn. She and Henry greeted all the church folks and then walked to the car. They got in and sat in silence while they waited for the car to warm. Hannah clutched her coat to her to warm herself. Henry rubbed her hands, "You and your icicle hands". Hannah smiled and looked out the window at the bare trees that lined the way. She remembered when she was thirteen and eavesdropped on her Mama and Mrs. Rosie's conversation that Sister Olive was having trouble conceiving. When they got home she had asked her mama why Sister Olive couldn't have a baby.

"Just ain't time for her yet."

"Can't she just pray and ask God for one?"

"Yes, and God will give her a baby in due time."

"Doesn't he see how much she want a baby though?"

"Child, you always ask too many questions." She went to the window and motioned for her to come. "Look out there."

"Just a tree."

"You see how that tree is bare?"

"Yes, mama. It *is* winter."

"Girl, don't get smart with me. Well, do you think that that tree could just start budding right now in December?"

"No."

"And why not?"

"It's not spring."

"Yeah, so it'll start budding in spring. Why? Cause that's the season for those things." She touched her under chin. "Everything happens in its season."

Hannah now rubbed the back of Henry's hand affectionately. They'd been home all winter and maybe having a baby would help her with missing her mama and Mrs. Rosie. A baby girl. And she'd name her after her mama and Mrs. Rosie. She looked at Henry and slid her hand to his thigh. He looked at her with a smirk on his face.

She kissed him, nibbling on his bottom lip. "Dear, the kids outside might see," he said, amusement filling his eyes.

"Then hurry up and get me home."

"You're gonna have to stop rubbing me, before we definitely give these church people something to see."

Hannah laughed and moved her hand. Henry put the car in drive and began to drive home. Both of them continued to steal glances at each other during the five-minute drive home. Henry looked over at her. *Wait until I get you home.* Hannah smiled and leaned to the right to rest her head on the window. She trailed her left index finger against the line of her neck. *You're not the only one with tricks.* Henry raised his eyebrows and chuckled. He nodded to himself. *Well, all right looks like I've got my hands full when we get home.* She pulled the pins out her hair slowly and then looked down at Henry's hands fidgeting on the steering wheel, she raised an eyebrow and bit her lip. *You're giving yourself away.* Henry rolled his eyes.

They pulled up to the house and Henry stopped the car. He looked outside whistled and looked back at Hannah. *You sure you don't want to do it in here?* Hannah shook her head no. Henry sighed with disappointment and then braced himself before he opened the door. Hannah felt the chilly air hit her, and she opened her door. Henry was on his way over to her side and he threw his hands up in the air. *God, Hannah, not even in freezing weather will you let me open the door for you.* Hannah winced. *Sorry.* She went back in the car and closed the door. Henry came up by the door and laughed. She spread her palms and presented the closed door, signaling him to open it. He opened the car and looked at her for a few moments before scooping her out the seat. She giggled and burrowed her face in his coat to keep it out the wind. He set her down when they got to the patio and fidgeted in his pocket for the keys and fumbled to open in the door. He turned to Hannah quickly and she smirked. *You're in a hurry aren't you?* Henry shook his head and chuckled and finally the door opened.

He let her go in and then closed the door behind himself. By the time she turned around to meet him, his lips pressed against hers. His lips were still cold, but the kiss was slow and lulling and she cupped his cheek. He twitched slightly and she mumbled that she was sorry for her cold hands. He took off her coat and she responded by kissing him and pulling his shirt out his trousers. She loosened his tie and began to undo the buttons on his shirt. She motioned her head towards the yellow couch with the quilt. *Let's go before we freeze.*

After, they lay under the large quilt on the couch. Henry cleared his throat under Hannah.

"My, my, someone was eager today."

Hannah smiled. "Stop."

"Stop what? You were the one being scandalous and trying to get us chastised by the church, then get us in a car accident. All cause you can't keep your hands off me. Shame on you Hannah."

He chuckled and Hannah joined in. The house was chilly and Hannah snuggled closer to him for warmth. "Henry, are you ready to have a baby?"

He rose up and rested his back against the arm of the couch. "I don't know...Are you?...Did you do all this to get pregnant?"

Hannah played with the hair on his chest. "No, not only for that."

"But, it was a big reason."

She still kept her concentration on his chest. "Maybe." She finally looked up at him. "I just think I'm ready now. I want babies."

"What happened to waiting a year? You said that, not me."

"Well, we've been married now for four months and even if I get pregnant now, then the baby will come a year after we've been married."

"I'd be happy to give you babies Hannah. You know that. But, there's the house that needs to be built, and I just got this job. Maybe we should wait until I get more settled before we start having mouths to feed."

"So what are you gonna do? Stop sleeping with me?"

"No. Maybe wear a rubber or just be careful. I don't know."

Hannah got up and headed to the stairs leaving him under the quilt. He called after her, but she stormed up them. She went into his mother's room and closed the door knowing that he wouldn't want to come in there. She was pulling on some clothes when he knocked and then opened the door, his chest bare with his trousers on.

"Come on, don't do that. Just talk to me."

She continued to do up the buttons on her housedress.

"Hannah."

"I want to have a baby Henry. I want something to look forward to after all that's happened."

"We just got married! That wasn't enough?"

"Of course it was wonderful."

"Then why all of a sudden do you want to change everything with this baby stuff?"

"Look, if you don't want to have a child, then just say so."

"Hannah, I never said that, and that's not the way I feel."

"Then what!"

"I just don't want you making a rash decision!" He sat on the bed. "A child changes a lot of things Hannah. It's not just about a baby smiling and being cute."

"I know that."

"Are you ready for your life to change?"

"Yes."

He rubbed his head. "Well, you might be ready, and I want

to make you happy, but, please Hannah can you give me some time? I need time to figure this thing out. We had good mamas. You know how to be a good mama cause you got to see them do right by us every day. Neither of us have a father. I don't know how to be a father."

Hannah sighed and sat next to him. "I didn't think about that." He didn't respond and she rested her chin on his shoulder. "I'm being insensitive. Just thinking about myself."

He glanced over at her with those celadon colored eyes. "Yeah," he said, amusement in his eyes.

She shook her head and smiled. "Is there anyway I can make it up to you?" she said, lightly letting her lips linger by his ear.

"Are you seducing me again?"

"If you want me to."

"What would be your motivation this time?"

"To let my husband know just how sorry I am. To show my husband how much I appreciate his patience with a headstrong 20th century woman."

"Can your husband get some biscuits after to renew his strength?" He said, pulling her onto his lap.

"Whatever he wants."

Hannah heard the rustling of the wind blowing the trees, and opened her eyes to the dark interior of Mrs. Rosie's room. She turned over and reached for Henry, but instead felt the emptiness there, and rose up groggily. She tiptoed out of the bed and checked the bathroom to see if he was there. It was then she saw the shadowy movement near Henry's room and peeked in. His back was to her, and he was holding that old, blue tattered shirt. His face was clouded by the darkness, and she stayed back so that he wouldn't see her. Hannah remembered the first time he'd shown it to her, and she'd wished she had something to hold onto from her Daddy. But, her mother had been one to leave the past in the past and holding onto his old things would only cause her pain. She'd always said that all she needed to hold onto was her daughter. Her mother never had a ring because they couldn't afford one. At least Hannah had gotten a simple gold band that matched Henry's. Hannah watched Henry as he held that shirt tight, and she tiptoed back to the Mrs. Rosie's room. She lay there thinking of Henry with a baby girl in his arms, that he'd hold her the way he'd held her these past few months. She heard him close the drawer and heard his footsteps come back into the room. He lay back down and wrapped his arm around her.

"It will be fine, you'll see," she whispered.

He didn't say anything, just kissed her temple and exhaled loudly.

Spring came with its pink blossoms, the ducks, and even the loon with its maniacal laugh returned back to the lake. Hannah stood in the kitchen, frying sausages and looking outside at the blooming flowers. They had started speeding up the work on the courthouse and the school, now that the ice had thawed. Hannah even suspected that Henry was at work with the new house, but he wouldn't tell her. He tried every excuse to keep her away from the land. She would've just snuck over there to peek, but fatigue seemed to rule her days. She hadn't even made the trip to see Pete or Mr. Cooper in a while, because she'd just spend her days napping the time away. Henry came downstairs, and Hannah scooped the sausage into a plate, and set it on the table. He gave her a peck on the cheek and sat down at the table and began to eat.

"Aren't you gonna eat?"

"I had a cup of tea. The sausages make me feel sick."

Henry chewed slowly and eyed her. "Are you-"

"Maybe. I'm not sure."

He grinned. "Well, go ahead and make sure before I go and get myself excited."

"Are you really excited?"

"Not yet, I don't know if you're having a baby."

"And if I am, you'll be excited?"

"Why wouldn't I be excited to have my boy?"

"*Fille*, Henry. It's going to be a girl."

Henry wiped his mouth and cleared the table. "Uh huh."

Hannah rolled her eyes as he moved to the sink. She stood next to him as he began to wash the dishes. "I know we weren't in agreement with it the first time. Are you sure about this?"

He smirked and she saw the light illuminate his eyes. "It may be a bit too late to start questioning that."

"I know, but I just…"

"Just what?"

"You've been doing a lot for me since everything happened. Too much for me."

"You're my wife."

"I know. I guess I just want to know what *you* want."

He scrubbed hard on the plate to get the grease off. "I'm not sure what you mean."

"You take me to church and you stay, even though you hate church. You change your mind about this baby. You cooked and cleaned for me for months and you don't go out with friends, not even Robert. I know I should think I'm the luckiest woman and I shouldn't ask these questions, but I want to know if this is what you want. Are you happy?"

He turned off the water. "You think I'm unhappy?"

Hannah fidgeted with her nails. "Sometimes I'm not sure."

"I'm happy Hannah."

"I can tell you miss them still. I know, and it's my fault they're gone. That's why I want to make it up to you."

He dried his hand on the towel and cradled her face. "It's not your fault Hannah. Please think rationally."

Hannah moved his hands and faced the window. "Who started the fire Henry?"

"I'm not going to do this with you again."

"Because you don't want to admit it!"

"No, because it's pointless!" He rested against the kitchen counter. "If I entertain that ridiculous thought that you killed our mothers, what then?"

"At least it'd be the truth! At least the blame would go to the right person!"

"And if I said I blame God, what would you say?"

"What do you mean?"

"The *almighty* God. What if I said I blame him?"

"You can't blame God, Henry."

"I can and I will."

"That's just pointless. Doesn't change anything."

"Yes, and blaming yourself doesn't change a damn thing Hannah."

Hannah could feel her face flush with heat and she looked away from him to keep the tears at bay. "I just want to make things better for you."

He pulled her to him. "And how do you plan on doing that?"

"The baby. I think having a baby will make this house happier."

"A life for a life. Hannah that's not in your control."

Hannah ran her hand over her stomach. If she couldn't control it, then God would. And she would pray and pray until he granted her children, her happiness and her life back.

Hannah looked out at the green landscape of the Michigan countryside as she buttoned her shirt. Henry had left for work early this morning. She was tired of staying in the house all day, and she left the house to walk to Pete's. It was a long walk, but the exercise was good. When she reached Pete's she stepped inside, but she saw no one there.

"Pete!"

He peeked out from the back and whistled. "Miss Hannah!"

He come over and gave her a quick squeeze, before he found his position behind the bar. She'd missed him. She knew that Henry had probably come to see him often, but she'd only seen him in passing for the last few months.

"How you doing? How you holding up?"

She took some peanuts from the jar. "I'm doing alright."

"Well, you don't look as frail. I know you women are always watching your weight, but you even look like you put on a few pounds."

Hannah laughed. "Yes, hard to keep off weight when you're pregnant."

Pete smiled. "Yes, your husband told me about a week ago. The boy's pretty excited."

"Is he really?"

"Yes, ma'am." He looked at her a few moments. "Come on, tell me what's going on."

Hannah sighed. "I know I've been a bit difficult to deal with."

"Why is that?"

"I just..." Hannah felt the tears choking her words. "I feel so bad for what I've done. I know he doesn't want me to blame myself, but I still feel like it's my fault they're dead. And I'm just trying to make everything better, but I don't think I am."

Pete patted her hand. "Stop trying so hard. Henry loves you."

"Does he tell you how he feels about being a father?"

Pete rubbed his hand across his forehead. "Hannah, every man is nervous about being father. I won't tell you the things he said, but I will tell you this. He said he's not signing up for no draft to be taken away from his wife and child. He's also working on that house like the dickens so he can give you something you dreamed of."

Hannah wiped at her eyes. "I guess we're both trying to make up for the past." She pushed some peanuts into her mouth. "Pete, I want you to be the godfather of my children."

Pete nearly choked and started coughing. "Don't you mean grandfather?"

Hannah laughed. "Whatever you feel comfortable letting them call you is fine. But, I want you to be the godfather."

"Of all of them?"

"Every last one."

Pete wiped at his forehead with a handkerchief. "Oh lord, Miss Hannah you really trying to take away the few black hairs I have left on my head."

"I won't force you, but I will say, that I can't imagine anyone else."

Pete looked at her and tapped his fingers on the counter. "You sure about this?"

"Positive."

"You talk to Henry about this?"

"Not yet, but I will as soon as I see him. And I'm sure he'll agree with me."

"Alright..."

Hannah grinned.

"Child, you are spoiled rotten."

June came and so did the tourists with their noise and bustling about. Henry had just finished work on the hotel. The hotel was beautiful, a stone building, which was uncommon in Idlewild. Their house was still in progress. Hannah had snuck off to the area a couple of times to see the wooden structure stretching up into the sky, and Henry and his men hammering and sawing away. She'd smile, as she'd see him there working himself into a sweat. She'd just stay there in the woods and watch them work sometimes. Henry hadn't caught on until he saw the mosquito bites on her skin. He just shook his head and said he should've known she would find her way out there. She'd had to promise she wouldn't go back and peek until he was ready to show her. Hannah's belly had taken its round form. It was pretty big for someone who was only three months along. She loved the way Henry would rub his hand against the roundness of her stomach and even talk to the baby. Sometimes he would sing to the baby old jazz standards and Hannah had taken to singing the songs from church around the house. The baby would often hear "Tis So Sweet to Trust in Jesus", even Henry had grown to like the song and sometimes she'd hear him humming or whistling it to himself.

She was waiting for him on the porch today, fanning herself with a folded piece of paper. He drove up and she smiled as he exited the car and came over to her. He sat on the chair next to hers.

"How was your day?"

He sighed. *Long.*

She moved behind him and began to rub his head. "I made some lemonade today. I'll get you some." Hannah went inside and got the pitcher from the dining room table. It was then she felt cramping under her stomach, almost the same cramps that came when she used to have her monthly. She closed her eyes for the slightest moment before another cramp rippled through her, it hurt so bad that she dropped the ceramic pitcher. She heard Henry ask if everything is ok, but then she saw the crimson staining her housedress. Henry barged in the house and all she could do was look up at him. They both didn't say a word for a long time.

Twins they said. They were two little twin girls. So small they could fit in your hand. It was a hemorrhage and having another child would cause more complications. Rest. Just rest. *Maybe* in a few years she would heal enough to have another child. You're young so there's still a chance for conception. No intercourse for eight weeks. We will give you something for the pain and the bleeding. *Will you give me something for the pain in my heart?* Stay off your feet for a while. Would you like to see a chaplain? Do you want to bury the children?

Two months. Two months of tears, two months of staying locked up in that house, two months of snapping at Henry and having him snap back. Two months of hell. The cool air that came with autumn was now starting to blow at nights and Henry would stay out late now to avoid her. They couldn't make love, so most times they would resort to arguing over Henry not putting down the toilet seat, about how she was too lazy to do anything around the house, about how much sunlight to let in the house. She decided to walk to Pete's tonight, the cool air on her face. As she neared she could hear the blaring music. She peeked in and saw Pete around the counter serving drinks. No Henry. She dipped back outside and stood there considering whether to go home or to go inside.

"Hello...sweetness."

Hannah turned to see a drunk, middle-aged man sitting against the side of the building. She eyed him warily. He hadn't shaved in a few days, his hair was tousled, and he was sweating despite the coolness.

"Hello," she said, looking around for anyone.

"I don't bite miss."

"Where are you from?"

"Detroit."

"Are you in the automobile business?"

"Yes ma'am. I screw one thing on the line three hundred times a day."

Hannah moistened her lips with her tongue. "I'm sorry sir. I understand when life gets hard."

"What does a pretty girl like you know about a hard life?"

Hannah put her hands on her hips. "Plenty."

The drunk passed her a bottle. "For your troubles." She was

going to tell him that she didn't drink, but instead she took that bottle and held it to herself.

"You should go to your hotel and get some rest sir."

"I haven't slept a full night in so long."

"Neither have I," she whispered.

He beckoned for her to give him the bottle and he snapped it opened for her. She sat down next to him and began to drink the bitter beer. She swallowed it fast and kept drinking. She finished and then asked for another, and another, feeling herself growing warm and unsteady. Then she heard Pete's voice.

"Hannah, where are you?"

She moved to hide from him and that's when she began to throw up.

The car was throttling her head around, she opened her eyes and Henry was there, his hand gripping the steering wheel tightly.

"You're up now."

Hannah stayed silent and braced herself for the fight coming.

"Hannah, what the hell were you doing drinking? Have you lost your mind?"

She stared out the window.

"Answer!"

She inhaled loudly and Henry slammed on the brakes. He parked the car, turned it off. Darkness surrounded them, and the sounds of the insects hummed around.

"I don't understand Hannah. You go out and get completely drunk. Do you know how hard that makes it for me to not want to go out and get something to drink? And plus, your health Hannah! You just had a miscarriage!"

"I know that! I don't need you to remind me!" She tried to open her door, but he reached over and locked it.

"You're gonna talk to me. We're not gonna run away from each other or the memories anymore."

"Shut up! You don't know what it's like to have something grow inside of you, and then have it taken away."

Even in the moonlight, Hannah could see Henry's temples tense. "That's always your excuse. That I don't know how it feels."

"Cause you don't."

He rested his head on the steering wheel, looking exhausted. "Sometimes you make it so hard for me to love you."

Hannah felt the tightening of her chest at his statement. "It's hard for me to love you sometimes, too."

His head still resting on the steering wheel, he turned his face to meet hers and then chuckled. "You can't do that. You gotta make your own comebacks."

"That isn't funny."

"Maybe not, but I must tell you Mrs. Carrington that even though I'm mad at you, that your lips are tempting me."

"You only want to kiss them to taste the liquor on it."

"Perhaps."

"Should I remind you, they may taste like vomit?"

He chuckled again. "Thanks for the reminder." He rose up and looked out the window. "I don't believe in separation in marriage. We'll work this out, we'll find happiness again."

"What makes you say that?"

"Faith."

Hannah turned and examined his face in the car. "I get what I've always wanted...you to believe in God, and now *I* don't know where he is."

"You'll find him."

"*If* he's even there."

Henry sighed. "Hannah, I can't argue now, I'm emotionally exhausted and I'm desperate for a drink." He rubbed a thumb over her bottom lip. "I'll tell you what, we'll go home, wash up and make love. I think that waiting for these two months is driving us both insane. Or, we can drive back to a bar and drink ourselves into a stupor. Your choice. I'll do either one."

She looked into his green eyes that looked almost translucent the way the moonlight was hitting them. "Drinking myself into another stupor is quite tempting, but the vomiting isn't that pleasant."

"No, it's not."

"I'll be angry when we make love tonight."

"So will I."

Hannah wondered, What would it be like to conceive a child in anger? What would that child be like?

"I'm not doing this to get you pregnant."

"What makes you think that's what's on my mind?"

"My dear, I know you."

Hannah smirked. "Drive home."

As he turned the key in the ignition and began to pull off, Hannah held back these words, "If you knew me so well, then you'd know that I don't care what you say."

They were so peaceful nowadays. So peaceful. They didn't even raise their voices, they weren't supposed to. That's exactly what they agreed on when Hannah found out she was carrying again. They were only to raise their voice to sing or to laugh. They would give this baby peace for the entire pregnancy. They began to overlook frustrations, like when Hannah smelt that faint smell of gin on Henry's breath when he said he'd been out late for work. Or when Henry had to just close his eyes and remember to breathe when Hannah had thrown his dinner out the window in retaliation for him coming home late with the groceries. Hannah knew it was unhealthy the way they treated each other. She'd noticed that Henry was drinking again, and she thought quite possibly having an affair. But, she couldn't, she wouldn't ask him about it. She didn't want to hear if he was. That would hurt too much. That could cost her this child.

Pete seemed to be the only sanity in their marriage. They'd begun to invite him every Sunday for dinner. They needed him to fill in the silence at the table. Soon he was there nearly every day either for breakfast, lunch, or dinner depending on his schedule. Once or twice, he'd tried to talk to Hannah about their marriage, but Hannah only told Pete that she wasn't going to discuss those matters. Hannah's stomach and feet swelled as time went by and soon walking to town became impossible.

In her last month, Henry moved them to the new house, the blue house with five bedrooms and the tub she'd always wanted. The house had polished wooden floors and tables, and the staircase had been sanded to perfection, with a rose design on it. She kissed him and thanked him for everything he had done, but she could see the slight reservation in his manner in the way he'd grown so silent and solemn. She had asked him to paint the interior in beige, except for their bedroom, which would remain blue. Blue made him happy. The rest of the house she decorated in green accents.

Hannah now sat in the tub soaking, it was evening when Henry walked in.

"You're home early," she said.

He sat down on the edge of the tub. "Didn't feel like staying out tonight. Wanted to come home to my wife."

"Your mistress isn't keeping you satisfied, I see."

"Mistress? What mistress?"

"The reason you stay out late so often."

Henry rubbed his face and groaned. "Hannah, you thought I'd taken a mistress?"

"What else was I supposed to think? Especially with you drinking again."

"My dear, the drinking is your fault. Ever since you came home drunk, the smell has stayed with me."

Hannah avoided his eyes. "So where were you? If you're not

with a mistress."

"At the lake, it's just a stone throw from the house. You'd know where I've been if you'd get out the house." Hannah rolled her eyes. "I'll sleep off the booze sometimes, read the paper, mourn the woman you used to be."

Hannah moved the water in her hands. "You could do that here."

"It's not the same."

It was then that Hannah began to cry for the first time in nine months, the tears ran down her face to her neck and fused with the bath water. "Do you love me anymore?"

Henry took the washcloth and began to run it over her shoulders. "I do. I just wish you were the woman who was alive and not this dead person." He ran the washcloth over her stomach that was sticking out from the water. "This child will need a mother who feels, who actually smiles, who laughs, who gets angry too."

"You're not the man I married almost two years ago."

"Who am I, then?"

"You're much better. Maybe you've turned into your father."

Henry smiled and rested his head on hers. She ran her hand on his facial hair and kissed his lips. Then she felt the cramping course though her. She looked down for blood, but saw none.

"Is everything ok?"

"Yes, but we'll need the doctor Henry." She smiled at him. "You're about to be a father." Henry's eyes grew wide and she watched him race from the room. She heard him on the telephone, before he came back to her side reminding her to relax. Henry moved her from the tub to a bedroom. The doctor came in thirty minutes and by then Hannah's contractions were seven minutes apart.

"This child is impatient," Hannah said, in between deep breaths.

"Just like their mother," Henry said.

"I will get you for that later."

"Mr. Carrington, perhaps you'd like to step outside during the birth," Dr. Johnson said.

"No, I want him here, Doctor," Hannah said.

"Mrs. Carrington, I insist he go."

"And I insist he stay. It's my house, my labor, my husband. I want him here."

Dr. Johnson exhaled loudly and looked at Henry. "Doctor, with all due respect, I think you should listen to her," Henry said.

"Fine, stay. If you pass out, it's not my fault."

Hannah could feel the cramping ripping through her. *Please, don't let my child die again.* The doctor kept going down there to check her, and normally she would've been tense, but she was in so much pain, she didn't care that another man's hands were on her privates. She kept hearing the sounds of Henry reassuring her that everything will be ok, the sounds of him praying coupled with the doctors instructions. Nothing mattered except the moment he'd told her she could push and finally release the pressure that had been pressing on her. She heard that strong cry and saw the bloody baby, his hands balled into fists, screaming at the top of his lungs. The doctor placed him on Hannah's chest and she finally felt Henry's hand again on her shoulder. Henry kissed her hair and whispered in her ear, "What are we going to name him?"

"Benjamin," she replied. "His name is Benjamin."

And LOVE covers a multitude of sin

Benjamin

The heat was thick around me as I bolted the screw into the engine. Then another engine came down on the belt and I bolted in the same bolt. Over and over I did this. All day. I sighed loudly thinking of the long day I had ahead of me. My shoulder blades were tense, and my eyes burned from exhaustion. The consistent comments from the professors that it would be better for me to continue working at the factory instead of trying to be a lawyer made me say with ease that life was hard for Negroes, even in Detroit.

It was 1966 and six years had gone by since I had left Idlewild and left behind my big house with its view of the pristine lake. I now had a view of a street with a neon liquor sign from my apartment. Life had been easy back home, filled with lazy days of ice cream, fishing, and swimming. Only winter brought real hardship, and even then, the beauty of Idlewild blanketed by snow was enough to make you appreciate life. I'd made my promises to write when I went off to "Howard", to call if I needed help, but all those had gone up in smoke when I had broken into Daddy's safe and left in the night. I missed Idlewild, and that ache inside of me would appear at the strangest moments. I could hear Motown music and instantly think back to the first time I'd heard The Temptations at the Flamingo Club. I remember the women in their sequined dresses, eager for a date. Also, each time Granddad Pete would get on my case about going there. I had worked for Granddad Pete since I was fourteen and his business was always competing with The Flamingo and Paradise Club. Often, the other clubs won. His club eventually became a hangout spot for older people, which is why I used to take every opportunity to go to other clubs, and dealt with the complaining from him afterwards.

Being an only child in a five-bedroom house had been strange, but had afforded me all the space I needed. Sometimes, I would just juggle between the different rooms, sleeping in each until Mama converted one into a drawing room and the other into a guest room. I'd always asked why I didn't have any siblings. Mama didn't like talking about it. Her eyes would well up and she'd stumble for words. Daddy told me Mama had an accident before she had me and she'd still been able to have me, but the doctor told her it was best not to have anymore babies or she could die. If I know anything about Mama, I'm certain she tried anyhow.

Detroit had a lake and autumn trees, but it didn't match the quiet that covered Idlewild for majority of the year. Don't get me wrong, I love Detroit, the city life, the nightlife, but you know you're a long way from home when you accidently call a bartender Granddad Pete. I'd thought about writing him a couple times, but Mama would find out and take the first bus here.

"Carrington!"

I turned to see my supervisor, his hands balled up, charging down the factory for me. His face was just a few shades lighter than salmon, and I couldn't tell if it was from the heat, or if he was just angry. Then again, his face was always that color, like he'd been sunburned.

"In my office." He pointed towards the room that needed a better light bulb and a good scrubbing, dusting, and sweeping. I'd only been in there three times. Once when I was hired, and twice for under performing at the job, which had been due to staying up late studying. But, this looked like it might be the fourth and last time.

Sure enough, my boss let me go. He was tired of hearing my excuses that I had been up all night studying for a law school exam. He didn't care that I had to study twice as hard as all the other students to even be remotely respected by the faculty. Most of them were so eager to see me fail that slacking off wasn't even an option.

It was alright, I hated that job anyways. I got on the bus to Woodward Avenue. I had some time on my hands before school started, so I hopped off and decided to walk around in the Detroit Institute of the Arts before heading over to class. I didn't feel like confining myself to the library and it was too cold to sit outside. I walked into the large stone building with its columns and the inside had the high vaulted ceilings like cathedral. Daddy would've loved this. I wonder if he'd ever been here. He told me he'd come to Detroit once or twice on business.

Walking through the museum, I stared at the architecture, and then zeroed in on a few works, like the Egyptian sarcophagus and the African masks. When I got to the European paintings, Mama's face floated to my mind. She and Daddy had saved up and we'd gone on vacation to Paris the summer after my 16th birthday. Mama had always smiled, but she was grinning like a child when we'd arrived. She kept telling me in French all the places she'd go to when she was a governess here. Daddy just rolled his eyes, begging her to speak some English for Christ sake. It was something Mama and I would do often, especially when we didn't want him to know what we were talking about. He always fussed, but I secretly think he liked hearing us speak in French and every now and then we'd realized he'd begun to understand a new word.

The sound of someone sneezing broke my reverie. It wasn't a normal sneeze; it was stifled, like someone trying to avoid making too much noise.

"Bless you."

"I'm sorry."

She was a tall woman, a good seven inches taller than Mama. She wasn't a conventional beauty. Her skin, the color of sand and brown hair pulled into a bun like a spinster. Her clothes showed that she probably didn't have much money for shopping either. In fact as I looked, I could say I'd been with women better looking. But, her large eyes and sweeping lashes had me arrested.

"No problem," she said. "I've seen this painting too many times too count." A southern accent. I wondered where exactly.

"You're a fan of Monet?"

"Oh, yes, I wish they had more than just 'Gladiolus' here," she said, setting her eyes back on the painting of the woman in navy with the umbrella walking along the pathway of a garden with red gladiola. "I'm a fan of almost every artist here."

"Do you work here?"

She chuckled. "Oh God no, I wish. I've been coming here after every payday for a year. I just like looking at the art. I've memorized a lot of them so far. I'm hoping maybe I can memorize them all."

"That's ambitious. I'm pretty sure if you walked into the office and showed them how much you knew about the collections, they'd hire you."

She laughed. "Hire a Negro to work in the DIA?"

"Yes, why not?"

"Mr.-", she motioned to me to give her a name.

"Carrington. Call me Ben."

"Ben," she said, carefully. I liked how she said my name, it almost sounded as if she was saying *been.* "I'm not sure which part of the country you're from, but in these here parts and in the South, no one wants a Negro in certain positions."

"I'm from Idlewild, Michigan if you must know and they may not want a Negro in certain positions, but they'll have to get used to it."

She stepped back and smiled. "I'm Addie. Adelaide. Addie for short." She pushed out her hand for me to shake.

I took it. Her hand was rough, her shake firm. "Nice to meet you, Addie."

She turned back to the painting. "I've never heard of Idlewild before."

"Maybe one day you'll go. It's nice there."

"I can barely get myself around Detroit. I'm from Ft. Myers, Florida."

"You're a long way from home. Weather here must be brutal for you."

She chuckled and I swore those eyelashes were the prettiest lashes I'd ever seen. Why was I feeling romantic over a woman with passable looks, but a pair of captivating eyes? "Brutal doesn't begin to describe how I feel about the weather," she said.

"Addie, would you mind if walked with you through the collections? Maybe you can explain some of them to me? It would help you prepare for your job giving tours here."

She smiled slyly. "No, I don't mind. But Ben, you seem like a charmer, I think I need to be careful around you."

"Really?"

"Yes, really. I'm not a fool. You've probably charmed lots of women, probably some from places I've only seen pictures of."

I crossed my arms over my chest. She continued, "You sound smart. Educated. Your clothes are designer, but worn. So let me guess, rich family, but down on your luck?"

Wow. I chuckled. "Oh, you're good." The only thing she had left out was that I'd only been with those girls to prove to my friends, to prove to myself that I could get them.

She met my eyes. "Look, I'm not the sort that you want to have a fling with. I'm hardly your type."

"And what is my type?"

"Rich, educated, pretty little play things -not 5'7 women with calloused hands from scrubbing."

I grinned and looked at her thick hair that was pulled back. It was filled with wavy curls. She'd look better with her hair down. Not to mention if she'd stop wearing those horrible clothes.

"I've never been with a rough handed scrubbing woman who's tall enough to look me in the eye. But, I will tell you that I'm very interested in getting to know the one standing in front of me." I wondered what would happen if I told her there'd only been three girls. One was a white Parisian girl I'd bragged to all my friends about when I got back home. None of them believed me. So, the other had been a summer visitor from Chicago in her twenties who thought I was much older than seventeen. The last had been a student in undergrad here, who had nearly driven me insane with her clinginess. She had our wedding planned out after we had slept with each other, told me that I needed to meet her father right away to ask for her hand in marriage, and exactly what ring she had wanted. It had taken several times of me telling her I didn't want to see her ever again, for her to finally understand. Not that it had stopped her from slapping me and calling me a bastard.

Addie narrowed her eyes suspiciously. "Maybe we should get on with the tour," she said, turning from me.

I smiled. "Good. One day I'll take you to Paris and we'll see all the Monet's you can find."

She turned back around and stared at me, her brown eyes focused in on mine. "Are you a liar too?"

I leaned in close and whispered. "You may think I'm a charmer. But, I can assure you, I'm no liar."

Just a thief.

Addie worked as a cleaning lady for this cardiologist in Grosse Pointe. Black men weren't usually welcomed walking around in that neighborhood. Plus, we lived on the west side. So, I'd wait for her each day for her shift to end around eight o' clock at night. She'd meet me at the bus stop and we'd walk to her cousin- Miss Cecile's apartment, and I lived about five minutes away down the road from her. It had been six months since we'd first met, and although she'd turned down my requests for a formal date around eleven times, I was certain that the next time would be the charm. After four months we'd first made love one night after going out for ice cream. Even though she pretended it didn't matter, I knew a part of her felt guilty and she'd always made sure to go to church any day after we'd been together. I guess that was her way of asking for forgiveness.

I thought maybe I'd be able to move on after that, but Addie had me transfixed. Maybe it was the way I could still remember how her lips still held the taste of the orange sherbet that night. Or it could be that conversations with her never seemed dead. Even if we both spoke no words, we seemed content to just be in each other's presence. I couldn't call it passion, like how I remember Daddy saying he was going out of his mind thinking about Mama. It was just a sense of tranquility I felt with her that hadn't been there since I left home. I was addicted to that calmness I felt around her.

Even though she wouldn't call us spending time together dating, she loved getting ice cream with me and going dancing. It bothered me that she had more power over me than I had over her, or she could just be really good at hiding it. Maybe it was similar to the way I never said "love" to her, I assumed it was implied.

Her cousin was much older than her, and a real strict, church going lady who would remind me each time I visited that it was time I get myself right with the Lord. She'd also say, "Adelaide, don't be drawn away by that ungodly music and dancing, and Ben, you keep your hands to yourself." Addie hated her real name and I always thought to ask Miss Cecile how I could dance with Addie and keep my hands to myself, but I kept my mouth closed. I'd only laugh and tell her the Lord and I were fine, I was just taking a break from being in his house every week.

The air was frigid. It made you feel like someone had locked you up in a freezer. There was one more week until Christmas. I was standing by a light post waiting when I saw Addie approaching. I called for her to hurry up. She ran to meet me.

"Goodness, I feel like the cold is cutting into my skin."

"Wait until January and February."

"Oh God, I think I may move back to Florida."

"Ne dire pas ça s'il te plaît."

She stopped. "How much French do you know?"

I opened my coat for her to come and get shelter from the wind and she moved inside. We kept walking.

"I want an answer."

"Quite a bit," I said.

"Ben. Do you see why I won't date you? Six months and I barely know this stuff about you."

"You know a lot about me. You know my favorite foods. You know I'm studying law and-"

"Tell me why you're not going home to be with your family for Christmas. Tell me how you learned French."

I looked down at her face. She was shivering against me.

"I learned from my mother."

"Was she a Frenchwoman? Is that where you got those golden eyes from?"

I grinned. "The eyes probably come from my father's side. His are green," Addie looked intrigued. "My mother was born in Texas, she moved to Michigan as a child. She was a governess in Paris for a couple of years."

Addie's face was illuminated by the streetlight. "Wow. I can't imagine living in Paris."

"I promised I'd take you some day."

"And what do you know about getting to Paris?"

"Shouldn't be too hard, since I spent a summer there when I was sixteen."

She stopped walking. "Ben. Please tell me you're joking."

"I'm serious sweetheart."

"Oh God, what do your parents do for a living?"

"My father's an architect. Mother, a teacher."

"Is your father a good artist?"

"Not quite as good as you. But, I may be biased because I think you're cute."

"I think you flirt in your sleep Benjamin Carrington."

"I wouldn't have to flirt so much if you'd just call me your boyfriend already Adelaide Walker."

She rolled her eyes. We were nearing her cousin's house. "And why can't you go home?"

The cold air filled my lungs as we stopped in front of her cousin's house. "I stole from my parents."

Addie moved from under my coat. "What?"

"I was supposed to go to Howard for school. But, I wanted to go down south and work in the fight. I kept reading about Dr. King and the Southern Christian Leadership in the papers, about the sit-ins and boycotts, and I wanted to be a part of that." I licked my lips and pushed my hands in my pockets. "But, I couldn't tell my parents, my mom would've lost it if she found out. She said I was crazy for wanting to leave paradise to go down there and be called a nigger. She was scared I would go down there and get myself killed. I'm her only child, and she never lets me forget it." Addie was shivering in the cold, although she made no moves toward me for warmth. I continued, "And my father, well, he was always too busy trying to keep me in line and make me a man of God, to listen to what I was trying to say about it. So I had them believe I was leaving for school, and I planned to maybe go to Morehouse instead. But, then I decided to stop off in Detroit just for a little to plan my way properly. But, I got spooked from going south when I heard all the horror stories from people here. But, I couldn't go home after what I'd done to them."

Addie sighed loudly and I saw the plume of cold air exit her mouth. She looked down at the ground for a few moments. Then her gloved hand reached mine. "Come inside there's something I want to show you."

I peeked inside. "Cecile will kill us."

"She's at a church revival."

"Oh I see."

She giggled. "Oh, no you don't, Ben. We're not sleeping with each other tonight. I just want to show you a painting."

"Is that all you want to show me?"

"Behave, before you get shown the door."

"Alright, alright, I'll be good." I smiled, she moved to go to the door, and I placed my arm on hers. "I'm not the womanizer you think I am."

She cocked her head to one side.

"I've been with women, but not many," I clarified.

"How many?"

"God, Addie. You really wanna know that?"

"I do." Addie wasn't reserved about these things. She'd told me about the boy back in Fort Myers that she'd spent a summer with and had promised her jewels and gowns. As the summer closed, he took back those promises and high-tailed it to New York City. After that, she hadn't opened up to another man. She'd satisfied her urges when the time was right, no strings attached, and she moved on.

"Three."

"Only three since you been in Detroit?"

I looked away embarrassed. "One, since I've been in Detroit. That was a couple years back. Been too busy for a woman, until you."

"Are you lying?"

"I told you, I'm no liar."

She pursed her lips and tilted her head towards the door. "Come on."

We walked up the front porch steps and Addie fumbled with the keys in the cold before getting inside. She sighed with relief as she entered. "Hurry and shut the door, before you let that cold air in."

I closed the door and began removing my scarf. The house was cozy, with old furniture that had been most likely bought at a consignment shop. You'd never be able to tell the way Addie and her cousin took pride in keeping the place spotless. I'd been in this house many times, but always with her cousin present. It looked clean as always, but the house felt so vacant with the absence of Cecile and her nagging. I followed Addie into the dining room and sat at the table.

"I'm gonna go upstairs and get it," she said.

I nodded. A Bible lay on the table. It was similar to the one that remained on the table at home, its burgundy cover a stark contrast to the blue of the tablecloth. Mama once told me that there was a time when Daddy didn't even seem to believe in God. Those days are hard to imagine. It wasn't as though he constantly shoved it down my throat. It was more that following in his footsteps seemed too great of a task.

Daddy did almost everything right. Mama lost her temper, Daddy calmed her. The only mistake I can recall was when he'd accidentally smashed his finger with a hammer as we worked on a new table for the drawing room. He'd cursed, and then apologized to me for doing it. I was eleven. I wanted to tell him it was fine, in fact a part of me wanted him to do it again, just to see more of his humanity. If I had a kid, I'd want them to see me as human and not a comic book hero.

I remember Granddad Pete used to tell me that Daddy used to be a womanizer before he met Mama. He also said that Daddy hated church and God. I still find that hard to believe. Every summer, he and I would go down to the lake and he'd spend time teaching me things from the Bible. After, we'd both swim out in the lake, often competing against one another. He always had a better backstroke than me. I took up the Bible on Addie's table and turned to the last scripture Pa had shared with me. My lips moved along with the words.

Have mercy upon me, O God, according to thy lovingkindness: according unto the multitude of thy tender mercies blot out my transgressions. Wash me throughly from mine iniquity, and cleanse me from my sin. For I acknowledge my transgressions: and my sin is ever before me. Against thee, thee only, have I sinned, and done this evil in thy sight: that thou mightest be justified when thou speakest, and be clear when thou judgest.

I didn't finish the psalm. Closing the Bible and setting it back in its place, I stretched and yawned. As much as I would complain and pretend like those Bible studies didn't matter, sometimes I wish I could go back to them now and feel the water of Lake Idlewild lapping around me once more.

Addie came back down stairs with a book in hand. She turned to a page and set it before me. "It's Rembrandt," she said, as I looked down at a painting of a bald, thin man being embraced by a bearded man while others looked on. I looked at the red robes of the Father and the older brother in the painting, compared to the rags the younger son was wearing with his shoes that were falling apart.

I looked up at her. "It's called 'The Return of the Prodigal Son'," she said.

"I know this painting." I rubbed the bridge between my nose and brow and sighed. "Addie…"

"Look, one day you're going to return home, because both of us know that Detroit will never be home. You don't belong here Ben. But, no one can make you go back until you come to your senses." She cupped my cheek. "Maybe I've been no help. Both of us have fallen from grace."

"You sound like your cousin." I pulled her arm gently for her to come near. "Don't you dare kiss me," she warned. "We're in the house alone and if Cecile comes home and catches us she'll kick me out for sure."

"Then you can come stay with me."

"Not until we're married," she said, with a smirk. "I'm still somewhat traditional."

I rolled my eyes. "Yes, you keep reminding me," I said, smiling. I pulled the pins out her hair so that her poofy, curly hair would fall to her shoulders. "My mama would love that you won't move in with me. I won't tell her about the other stuff," I said, winking at her.

She pinched me. "Good, then you'll have to introduce me to her when we go to Idlewild."

"*We?*"

"Yes, we. I don't like living in the city either. Maybe a quiet life in Michigan will suit me. One where the only house I'll have to clean is my own."

"So we're getting married, going to Idllewild, and we'll have our own home?"

"Of course. Oh, and don't forget Paris."

"I haven't," I said, cupping her cheek. "So you've turned down all my dates, but you've decided all this?"

She smiled. "Have you ever promised a woman Paris?"

"No."

"Have you told anyone about your *thieving ways*?" she said, teasing me.

"No."

"Cause you don't talk to anyone really, but me. You're so quiet around everyone. Except with me." She reached out and touched my hair. "I'm just kidding Ben, you don't have to marry me if you don't want to. We can just live in the moment."

I looked into those big dark eyes. *She's lying.* "Hmm.. well, I'll have to think about all that," I got up and walked towards the staircase. "But, I can think of one way we can live in the moment," I said, pointing upstairs to her room. I held out my hand for her and she grinned and took it, pulling me up the stairs.

Christmas came with its flurries that melted once they hit they hit the ground. Addie told me she would be coming over after church. I looked at the clock. It was noon and I was in my kitchen, if I could even call it a full kitchen. My studio apartment usually lay in disarray, but Addie refused to see me if my place was a mess. She could spot dirt from a mile away. I had attempted to make some gingerbread, because Addie told me she loved it. My attempt failed. I left it in the oven too long and the bottom was completely black and charred. I scraped some of the burnt flakes into the garbage.

Both Mama and Daddy could cook and I could only make eggs and toast. Eating out was costing me a fortune. The radio news continued jabbering on about Walt Disney's death and the bombing of Hanoi. Meanwhile, trying to lift everyone's spirits by mentioning how successful the viewing of *How the Grinch Stole Christmas* was.

Someone knocked on the door. The familiar tune of The Supremes' "Can't Hurry Love" filled my room. Addie always knocked to that tune. I opened the door and she was standing there in a red dress that flared out at her waist. Her coat was draped over her arm.

"Merry Christmas," she said, giving me a peck on the mouth.

"Merry Christmas," I said against her lips.

She came in and put her coat on the hanger. "It smells like...burnt ginger," she said, removing her scarf and gloves.

"Correction, burnt gingerbread."

Addie rolled her eyes and laughed. "You tried to make gingerbread for me?"

"Anything for you, Miss Walker," I said, putting my hands in my pockets.

She gave me a ghost of a smile. "What's wrong?" I asked. She shook her head.

"Nothing." She moved to the kitchen. "What do you have in here? I could cook up something."

"No, no, no. Relax, I want this day to be about you. I want you to open your gifts."

"*Gifts?*" she grinned. "Ok, I'll cut the gingerbread while you get them."

I reached under the bed retrieving the wrapped presents. When I turned back around she was cutting the burnt ends off four slices of gingerbread. Her eyes went wide when she looked at the gifts that ranged in sizes. I handed her one. "Open this one first."

She looked at me with mock suspicion. "What are you up to? I don't think I've ever seen you this excited."

"Just open it."

She began to undo the wrapping and then pulled out the paintbrushes. Her face was bright with excitement.

"Ben-"

"Ahh, next one," I said, handing her another box. She smiled at me like a child before ripping away at the wrapping. Twenty-four colors of acrylic paint. "Where'd you get the money? I thought things were tight-"

"Open the last one." She didn't argue this time; she just stepped over to the large rectangular present and tore at the paper. She didn't even finish taking the paper, but just stared at the canvas underneath. She looked up at me and I noticed the moisture welling in her eyes. She hadn't even looked to see the easel and the paint tray.

"Why are you crying?"

"I should've gotten you something more thoughtful."

I cradled her face in my hands. "I'm sure you got me something nice. Don't worry about me."

Her tears dropped on my hands. "You're too good to me."

I smiled and dropped my hands down to my sides. "So what's this gift you're so worried about?"

"Well, there's two gifts," she said slowly. I raised an eyebrow. She went over to her coat and pulled out an envelope. I took it from her and opened to find a few bills inside.

"I saved back about $50. I figured it might help with your bills. I didn't want you to be without heat again." She looked at me trying to gauge my reaction. "I'm not sure how you feel about taking money from me, but know that I won't be accepting it back, so you might as well make use of it."

I burst out with laughter. "I figured you'd say something like that." I walked over and kissed her forehead. I'd never thought

I'd be accepting money from Addie, but she wouldn't accept any talk of male pride. "Thank you, Addie, I really mean it."

She smiled shyly. "You're welcome."

"And the other gift?"

She swallowed. "Umm, how about I paint it on my new canvas?"

"Sure," I said. I went to my drawers and threw her an old shirt. "Wouldn't want you to mess up your pretty dress."

"Thank you," she said moving to the bathroom. "Get something to cover your floor."

I got some old newspaper and began to set it down when she came back in my old shirt and nothing else. "How do I look?" she said.

"Like my second Christmas gift."

She put her hand on her hip. "You need to take a nap."

"That wouldn't be so bad. But, it'd be better if you'd join me." I said, patting the bed.

"Nope. Sit back and relax while I paint."

I reclined on the bed and picked up a book of crossword puzzles. We sat there for a while, me figuring out the puzzles, asking her for help on occasion, while she sat there mixing paints on old newspaper, and then touching the paintbrush to the canvas. I wanted to go over and peek, but I knew she wanted this to be a surprise so I kept put.

"How much longer?" I asked.

She didn't look at me. "Give me ten more minutes."

I looked over at her. Her features looked tight and moisture lined her forehead.

"You need me to turn down the heat?"

"Why?"

"You're starting to sweat."

"I'm fine," she stammered.

I put down my book and sat up on the bed. I looked out the window at the grey sky. I reached for my torts book. I started to turn through the pages of that when I heard her rising from her chair. She stepped from behind the canvas and faced me. I smiled at how she looked with her hair a bit disheveled, paint smeared on her hands and my shirt. She pulled the painting off the easel and turned it around for me to see. The painting was of me, I could tell by the glasses, in the painting I was wearing a blue shirt and looking down adoringly at a baby in my arms.

My eyes flew to Addie's. She fumbled with her hands, but maintained eye contact with me. "Cecile began to suspect and sent me to the doctor. He confirmed it. Cecile kicked me out this morning."

I took a deep breath. "I don't know what to say."

"I know this isn't what you wanted-"

"It isn't."

She stilled at my words. She looked at me for a few moments and then stormed off to the bathroom. The slamming of the door brought me back to attention. I rose off the bed and went to the bathroom. The sink pipe was running. I knocked on the door. "Addie."

She didn't answer. I knocked again and she opened the door, now in her red dress. She threw my shirt at me and then went to the coat hanger to get her things. "Addie. Where are you going?"

"Somewhere."

She opened my front door and stepped outside. "You don't have anywhere to go," I said.

"I'll figure something out. I always have."

"Don't say that. Come back inside."

She turned away from me and went down the stairs.

New Year's had passed two days ago and Addie was still avoiding me like the plague. I'd gone to Cecile to figure out where she was, and gotten called a "godless, heathen man". Eventually, I'd gotten Cecile to give me two bits of information. Addie was one month along in her pregnancy and the name of her motel. I rapped on the door of the inn. No answer.

"Addie, open the door."

I heard rustling inside and then she opened. She was in a pair of bell-bottom jeans and a green sweater. I stepped inside of the moldy smelling room.

"Are you ready to talk about this?" I asked.

She pursed her lips and sat on the bed with its once white bedspread that had turned a soft yellow. "It's my problem, not yours."

I closed my eyes and breathed deeply. "The child is mine as well."

"I thought this wasn't what you wanted." Her eyes were welling up with tears.

"What did you expect me to say? I was in shock! I didn't plan for it to be...this way. But, since it is, I want us to be a family."

She snorted sarcastically.

"Let's get married like we said."

"You only want to get married because I'm pregnant,"

I moved and sat next to her on the bed. "I thought you knew I wanted to marry you. I want to marry you because I love you. Don't you love me?"

"But you'd meant *eventually*. Not *now*."

"So, I changed my mind. Let's do it now," I said, putting my arm around her and bringing her close to me. "But, Addie, you're going to have to say you love me. My parents had love in their marriage. I never expected anything less."

She looked down at the stained carpet.

"You like to be in control, and you never expected to fall in love with me. You thought I'd just be one of your flings."

"Are you using your skills as a lawyer to analyze me?"

"Maybe."

"How do I know you're telling the truth?" she said, pulling away. "How do I know you won't up and leave me? I don't want you to lie to me. I can raise my child on my own and leave you in peace. But, just don't lie and tie yourself to me if you don't love me."

I exhaled and then looked in her face. "You could never leave me in peace. You're the first time I've gotten a glimpse of it in years. I do love you Addie. Maybe I'm not as vocal about it as I should be, but I love you. I'm not going to leave you like those other men. I'm not the same and you know it, but you're scared. Answer the question. Addie, do you love me?"

She exhaled and rubbed her eyes. "Yes." I walked back over to her. She kissed me softly. "I have ever since you told me I was good enough to work at the DIA."

We got married in a courthouse downtown two days later. I thought maybe Addie would want a proper wedding and all, but she said that we didn't have the money. Plus, she wouldn't feel right having a big celebration without our families. Her parents were back in Florida and too poor to afford a ticket to come up here. Plus, they weren't too happy when they'd received Cecile's letter saying that she'd kicked the fornicating Addie out the house. Addie still called them and sent them pictures of us in the mail, at the steps of the courthouse, in her simple white dress and bouquet of white sweet peas. While they weren't happy with the way we'd done things, they sent their best wishes, and hoped we had tons of babies. Addie said she didn't want lots of babies, but that being a mother seemed nice. Addie was something else, I would always say to myself. I couldn't believe I'd actually had to argue with her that giving her a wedding ring was necessary. She'd just wanted the money spent on more art books, paint, and charcoal, and now she was thinking of going to college or becoming a "real" artist if I passed the bar tomorrow.

I was sitting up in bed, my glasses leveled on my nose, reading through a practice exam. I put down the exam on the wooden nightstand we had painted blue since it was the only color we could agree on. If it were up to Addie the whole apartment would be in orange and yellow. I put down my glasses next to the lamp. Addie was laying down beside me her hair falling all over her face. I pushed it back and kissed her cheek.

"I know you're not asleep," I said.

She smiled serenely, her eyes still closed. "Yes, I am."

I shook her softly. "Come sit with me for a little bit."

"You need to go to sleep. Big test in the morning."

I tickled her. "Adelaide Carrington. Come sit with your husband for a little while." She squealed as I lifted her onto my lap.

"One night I'll pay you back for this and keep you up all night."

"You already gave me enough sleepless nights."

"Really? When was that?"

"When you kept turning down my offers to be my woman."

She leaned back and laced her fingers between mine. "Good. Well, you got what you wanted in the end, so I shouldn't have to suffer."

I rested my lips against her soft hair, shiny with the coconut oil she'd put in it.

"Ben, you're going to do fine on the test."

"What if I don't?"

"Then you'll take it again. But, you wont have to, cause I know you'll pass."

"How do you know that?"

"Because you've been driving me nuts with every law in Michigan. I think I could be a lawyer, just from listening to you."

I laughed. "And you don't do the same thing with art to me? Did I not have to sit here for an hour while you painted me?"

She pinched me. "I thought you liked it."

"I do like it." I kissed her cheek. " I would've liked it better if you'd given me one of those nude paintings of yourself."

She shook her head. "You need to go to bed."

Addie turned to look at me. "What happens after this? After the bar exam?"

"I start practicing, maybe I can get a job somewhere where they'll give a Negro man a chance." Addie turned around and started playing with the ends of her hair, twirling it around her finger. "But, first, I'm gonna take you to Paris for two weeks."

"What?" she said, turning back around to see me. "Ben we don't have the money for that for right now. We need to use that money for the baby, this apartment, or-"

I started to run my hands over the curves of her body. "You sure you don't want to see the Eiffel tower? Or go to all those art museums?"

She sighed. "Stop that. I can't think clearly when you start all that."

"I don't want you to think clearly right now."

She moved my hands. "You have no choice."

"Let me make you happy Addie. I promised. You didn't want a wedding, I gave you that. Let me give you the type of honeymoon we should've had."

She turned to look at me. "How much will this cost?"

"Doesn't matter. I told you I wasn't a liar, so I'm going to take you there."

"And then after?"

"What do you mean after?"

She moved out of my lap and reclined back down in her usual spot. She pulled me close to her. "After, let's go home to Idlewild."

The room felt hot. She rubbed her thumb over my cheek. "Ben, it's gonna be ok."

"How do you know?"

"Because everything you've told me about Idlewild, feels like home."

I closed my eyes, as I felt her calloused hands on my face. "Adelaide."

"Benjamin."

"I need to get some sleep. We'll talk about this in the morning," I said, as I turned over. I could hear the rustle of sheets and knew that she was probably thinking of saying something. But, instead I heard the clicking of the lamp and then darkness enveloped the room.

Three hours of asking what are the rights of both parties. What are the rights of Patty, Kirk, and Frank? What legal arguments do I suggest and why? As I got out the exam I pondered back on all my responses. On my silence with Addie last night.

I can't go back to Idlewild. Not without Pa's two thousand dollars. Not without shame.

I had waited for them to doze off that night. I waited even longer than I thought I should, just to make sure they were sound asleep. Then I went downstairs my backpack in hand, careful not to make any of the steps creak, and into Pa's work room. He kept the safe in the cabinet by his pencils. He had told me the way to unlock it once when I was fifteen, just incase anything should happen to Mama and I had to become the man of the house. He told me about his old house a few minutes away. I could always go there if something went wrong. I heard the clicking of the safe as it opened and I grabbed what was inside. The deed to the house, which I put back, and two thousand in cash. I considered putting back some of it, but I would need all that money, combined with my five hundred I had saved up from working with Grandad Pete. That money lasted me a couple of months and then I'd taken to hustling people in pool and poker. No one suspected the quiet man with the reading glasses.

When they saw all the work I did with Dr. King, they'd understand, and I'd pay them back. I put the money in my backpack and left the house quietly. I walked twelve miles to Reed County to catch a bus, my chest feeling tight, missing my family already and wondering each moment if I should turn around, return the money and get back in bed. I should've at least left a note.

What did Pa and Mama look like now? Would their hair be all grey? Would their skin be leathery and sagging? They were only a little over fifty, maybe not. Could Mama still chop her own wood? And Grandad Pete? I didn't even know if he was still alive. If Grandad Pete had died, I wasn't sure I could forgive myself.

As I neared my apartment building, I braced myself for Addie. She probably would give me the silent treatment today, just as I had given her all morning before leaving for the exam. I entered the building shaking the cold from my coat. I walked up the dusty stairs that the landlord rarely cleaned. Sometimes Addie would come down and clean them just because she couldn't stand filth.

I pushed my key in the lock and opened the door. I slowly closed back the door. There were streamers and decorations, of course they were orange and yellow, against all that blue furniture we had gotten at a bargain from several yard sales. Addie stood there in her short dress that I liked with the brightly colored triangle pattern on it, her baby bump showing.

"Surprise!" she said, her smile bright.

"What's the occasion?"

"Your bar exam."

"You don't even know if I've passed yet."

She rolled her eyes. "Oh that doesn't matter. All that matters is that you did it. Come on, take that coat off and come here."

I smirked, eyeing her with suspicion as I took off my coat and put it on the hanger. "Did you do something bad, Addie? Something I need to fix?"

She folded her arms over her chest. "So I can't do something nice for you?"

I sat down and started to loosen my tie. "Of course you can, you do a lot of nice things for me. But-"

"No buts," she said, sitting on my lap. "I just don't want you to be mad at me anymore."

"Oh, so the silent treatment works with you? You have mastered every way to make me surrender, and now I finally know something that gets under your skin."

She pouted. "Don't be mean Ben." She played with the collar of my shirt. "You're quiet with everyone. Not with me. It makes me feel special to say that Ben talks to me all the time."

"Sorry for not making you feel special," I said, kissing her hand.

"Ok," she said, giving me a peck on the lips. "And don't let it happen again," she said chastising me while trying to hold in her laughter. "Do you want cake?"

I got up. "No, I think I want to dance with my wife first." I went to the record player and put on the Marvin Gaye's "How Sweet It Is". She smiled as I extended my hand.

"So I take it the test went well?"

"Yes, I think I did well."

"So, I'm going to be a lawyer's wife?"

"There's a good chance of it."

"Never in my wildest dreams, would I have thought I'd marry a handsome man like you with honey colored eyes. And a lawyer to boot, I did *good*."

I chuckled. "Did I tell you what I loved the most when I first saw you?"

"Oh God, Ben let's keep this discussion clean."

I laughed. "For once, my mind is not there, although I must admit there were many things to admire." Addie swatted my behind. "Look who's trying to start things," I said.

She eyed me. I lifted her face. "Those big brown eyes. With the long lashes."

She gave a shy smile. "That's sweet."

"I hope our daughter will have eyes like yours." They didn't know the gender, but Ben thought it was a girl. He could just feel it.

"You sure you don't want her to have your eyes?"

"I think yours are prettier."

"Well, we should know soon."

We danced all night to the record before we turned in for the night.

It was July 19, 1967 when the mail with the bar exam results came in the mail. Five months of an agonizing wait. All I did was listen to the news of Vietnam, complaints of how LBJ was handling the war, and as always I listened to the latest news of what Dr. King was doing. Tension seemed to mark my days, the same way the Detroit air seemed thick with it. Addie was convinced they weren't deliberating my test scores, but rather my skin color.

"Open it!" Addie was screaming, her face round from the weight gain. Eight months of pregnancy and she already looked like she could deliver any moment.

"I'm nervous!"

"Open it Ben!"

I took a deep breath and opened the envelope. *The Michigan Board of Bar examiners is pleased to invite you to the Ceremony...*

"I passed!"

Addie screamed and I lifted her up. "You're going to be a lawyer!" she said.

I let her down. "Ok, you're not as light as you used to be."

She pinched me and then smiled gently. "Your parents would be proud."

I sat down and she stood in front of me. I rested my hands on her growing stomach. "They would be." I moved my ankle around in my shoe that was worn down.

"They should know their grandchild," she said, playing in my hair.

I rubbed my hand over her stomach. "How will I face them?"

She kissed my hair. "With humility, my dear."

Glass broke outside. I felt disoriented from sleep, rubbed my eyes and sat up in the bed, reaching for Addie. The room was bright enough to see what was going on, since the liquor sign kept the room somewhat illuminated. Addie said groggily, "What was that?" Glass was smashed again, and along with that came the sound of a woman screaming. My heart began to beat fiercely. I could feel my heartbeat all over my body, the sound reverberating in my ears. Addie sat up fully. I moved out of the bed.

"Stay there," I said to her.

I went to the window and peered out. There was a mob growing outside. One white, one black.

"What's wrong?" Addie asked.

"Stay here. Stay away from the windows." I pulled the curtains and went to the front door and locked it. I grabbed a bat near the front door. *I knew I should've bought that gun when I had the chance.* I went back into the bedroom, baseball bat in hand.

"Ben you're scaring me."

The window broke and a flaming can sailed inside.

Addie's scream pierced the room.

The curtains caught on fire and I grabbed Addie up and moved her from the bed. I raced to the kitchen and filled a bowl with water, trying to douse the flames. Addie's eyes were wild with panic. She moved to the jar on top of the fridge. *Our savings of two hundred dollars.* She tried to gather some of her art books, sketches, and paintings. She fumbled to hold them all. I grabbed them up and told her to get out of the apartment. The art books tumbled to the ground, and I tried to shove the loose photos back inside, before my eyes grazed back on Rembrandt's painting. I tucked it away. I looked at the flames still licking at the curtains, now spreading to our bed. I hurriedly reached under the bed and grabbed the box under there. *Our wedding pictures, the menu from the restaurant we went to with friends afterwards, the letter from the Michigan bar, our memories.*

I headed outside of the apartment, my eyes roaming for Addie. I rushed down the stairs for her, she was standing off in the corner of the lobby breathing heavily, one arm clutching the money, the next clutching her stomach. No, this couldn't happen right now. The heat from the building was making me sweat all over. Red and blue lights flashed outside, sirens filled the air, and mass hysteria was growing. I pulled Addie outside into the night. Men were pummeling their fists into one another. Blood flowed from noses, mouths, and cuts. They were fighting a war in Vietnam, not America, and yet bodies were splayed out on the ground like soldiers in battle. Words like nigger, honky, and kike were thrown around like it was bombs flying overhead. Garbage cans loudly clanged as they were thrown at storefronts and people raced inside, filling their pockets with merchandise.

A police man approached us yelling, "Nigger you a part of this?!"

"No, sir."

He hit me with his nightstick across my back. I felt pain course through my body and heard Addie scream.

"I didn't do anything!"

He raised me up by the collar of my shirt and pummeled me in the face with his fist.

"Leave him alone!" Addie said, reaching for him.

"Look here, nigger gal, you better mind your own before I lock you up."

My body was wracked with pain. "Officer, please, she's pregnant."

"My husband didn't do anything! Who do you think you are calling us niggers, you bastard! My husband is a lawyer!" I could see the fury in Addie's eyes.

"Addie!" I yelled.

The officer turned to me. "So you're one of them uppity niggers, huh? Your wife's got a lot of mouth." He kicked me in my stomach. "I don't care if you're a lawyer." He sailed a punch in my face. "You're still a nigger." I raised my hand in defense. He grabbed my head and slammed against the concrete. The world seemed to explode with pain and then get fuzzy. Like when the antenna on the television leans too far to one side. "And do your best to remember that." He spit on me. "Now you two have a good night."

Mama was in my apartment. Just sitting there on the blue couch braiding her hair, like she's lived here all her life. I sat down next to her and she pinned her hair back into a bun. She studied my face.

"You look like your father."

"Is that a compliment?"

She gave that familiar grin, her smile almost making her eyes look like she was squinting. "I wouldn't have married him if he wasn't handsome. You have his looks, but, you have my stubbornness. "

The clock began to tick loudly while we looked at one another.

"I'm not sure if I can come back."

"Pourquoi ça?" Why not?

The ticking of the clock and the sounds of a radio began to fill the room. "J'ai perdu mon chemin." I've lost my way.

Mama held my hands. "Tu connais le chemin de la maison." You know the way home.

I woke up in a room that smelled like potpourri. The room was filled with dusty rose colored accents- the curtains, the bedding, and the decorations on the dresser. The sound of a radio filled the room. *Over forty dead, more than four hundred injured and seven thousand arrested.* I moved to turn it up, but my back ached with bruises. I groaned.

Addie was sitting in a chair nearby cradling a baby, its arm outstretched. She rushed over to the bedside. "I'm so sorry Ben. Me and my big mouth."

My head hurt. "You're not hurt are you?"

She was crying. "No, just a bit sore from delivering this little one." she said, putting her hand gently on my face. I winced. "You had a concussion. Lots of people are hurt. People are dying."

"You had the baby without me."

Addie gave a solemn smile. "I tried to wake you." She leaned over and showed me the face of a tiny baby girl, her color still hadn't come in, and she yawned and stretched before settling back into a dreamlike state.

I smiled and reached my hand to touch the rose petal softness of her hand.

"I was thinking we could name her Eden."

"Eden," I said, rolling the name over in my mind, while the images of home circled my mind.

"You hate it?"

"No, I love it."

I let go of Eden's hand and looked around. "Where am I?"

"A couple, the Robinson's, came and found us on the street, I started going into labor during the riot. The hospitals are full." A grandfather clock made a loud gong. "The Robinson's let us stay; she's a retired nurse. Mrs. Robinson is a godsend; she helped me deliver, while she gave her husband instructions on what to do for you. I don't think any of us would have survived without her. She's been taking good care of you."

"How long have I been out?"

"Three days."

Mama was right. I should've never left paradise for this.

Addie kissed my forehead. "We're gonna go home," I said.

"The apartment burned down, Ben."

"No, I meant to Idlewild. I'm ready to go home."

First, we had to both recover and settle ourselves with Eden before we could leave. The day I woke up, I held Eden in my arms and Addie and I have been competing for attention since. Her hair was black and silky, no curl to it, just straight hair that pointed in every direction until you smoothed in against her head. She would have my copper colored eyes, but I was grateful for the long lashes I could already see she had gotten from Addie. Now I understood why my father had been so perfect to me, because when I held Eden I wanted to be everything for her as well.

I couldn't give her that life here in Detroit. The life she deserved was the one I'd been given back in Idlewild. Pride couldn't stop me from giving her that life. No matter how hard it would be, I'd have to find my way back home.

The riots had destroyed most of the black businesses and there was already talk of people fleeing to other cities for refuge since hundreds of buildings were burned down. Addie hated hearing all that bad news on the radio, she just wanted to focus on Eden, and on getting to Idlewild. She was a good mother. I know she told me she'd cared for babies before, but she just looked natural in this role. I liked sitting and watching as she fed her and I'd had her teach me how to properly bathe Eden. I was grateful that I'd been able to save her art supplies, cause she'd painted a portrait of me holding Eden while sitting on the bed.

Two weeks later, we boarded the bus to Idlewild. The Robinson's had taken real good care of us and urged us to stay just a few more days, but I was ready to go. Mrs. Robinson had made sure Addie had some diapers for Eden, and blanket the color of pink bubble gum balls. She also made sure we'd gotten a suitcase to store our things, and that I was speaking, walking, and thinking coherently. She asked me the most ridiculous questions about history, my life, and math, just to see if my brain was all right. She'd smiled her approval at all my correct answers and said to Addie, "You got yourself a smart one."

At first, both of us didn't say much the entire ride. The swelling had gone down, but the cuts on my face and the bruising on my ribs and back still made me groan. The Robinsons let us borrow some clothes even though none of it fit, but it was better than going home in clothes with blood stains on them. I tried to pay them for taking such good care of us and for sparing their food, clothes, and water, but they wouldn't take a dime from us.

I would be coming home with only $200 to my name. Ten percent of what I owed Pa. I had wanted to pay him interest for what I had taken. The lump in my throat felt thicker as we neared. I felt sick as we hit the town of Chase. Addie spent most of the time looking out the window marveling at the countryside, talking softly to Eden wrapped in her pink blanket, and trying to conceal feeding her on the bus, while people looked on. The grass was just as I'd remembered; it seemed to just go on. We used to play soccer and baseball, being careful to leave once the white kids got there or we'd be sure to get beat. Addie would turn ever so often to smile at me and then rub my arm reassuringly.

The bus let us off at Baldwin Road.

"I'll find someone to drive us to the house," I said to Addie.

"Is it far?" she said rocking Eden.

"No, about a fifteen minute walk."

"Then I'd like to walk."

"Addie, you just gave birth."

"And you're beat up," she fired back. "Mrs. Robinson said walking is good," Addie said. "Please? It's so beautiful, I don't want to miss anything."

I started to walk and she laced her free hand in mine. "You're sweating Ben."

I smirked. "Stop teasing."

"I'm not teasing," she said, and looked off in at the trees in wonder.

I breathed in the cool air. The temperature was much cooler than Detroit's, the air absent of the smoke, the atmosphere void of the sounds horns. I wasn't used to Idlewild being so vacant during the summer. Things had changed. All that could be heard was the whooshing of the trees, the pitter-patter of the leaves against the tree bark, the pecking of the woodpecker, and occasionally Eden's whimpers before she settled down again. As we neared, I looked at the blue house that I'd grown up and I froze with fear. I saw the canoe Daddy and I would take out on the lake and fish with. The tree stump Ma used to chop wood and my eyes roamed over the lake that Daddy had taught me to swim in, the lake Mama would take me by to teach me French.

Addie turned to look at the house and then at me. "Ben it's ok. Ben." The sound of the screen door opening filled the air, that thing always needed oiling. A small woman, her skin dark, her features still young, but her eyes had wrinkles by the edges that gave away her age. Grey hair mingled with the dark hair she had framed around her face. Mama. Another dark old man stepped out, barely able to walk without his cane. Granddad Pete.

"What's wrong with you Hannah?-"

Then I saw the tall cream-colored face man, his eyes still that solemn green, peer out the door. He was wearing a crimson colored shirt, tucked into some khaki pants.

"Ben?" it was just a little louder than a whisper.

"Who's Ben?" Granddad Pete said, and I realized the old man I'd left here had gotten much older, as he looked on at me with confusion. Mama touched him reassuringly and whispered something to him before he responded loudly that Ben was only fifteen and worked for him, not this man.

Daddy kept his focus on me. Then he ran. He ran to me. "Ben!" He called.

He stopped right in front of me and I tried to pull myself together so I wouldn't sob right then and there. But, the unshed tears burned my eyes and nose. Grandad Pete would never know me again, would never understand that I was sorry. I dropped to my knees. "I'm sorry, I'm so sorry. I brought some of the money back," I mumbled.

"I don't want your money, son."

"I have to give it back," I said, fumbling in my pockets for the money.

He shook my shoulders. "Ben, you're home. That's all we wanted."

He looked up at Addie. "I take it, you're his wife."

I turned around. Tears were streaking her cheeks. "I am."

"And I take it you're holding my grandchild!" Mama called from the door.

Addie laughed. "Yes, ma'am I am!" Addie shouted back.

"Ben stop your blubbering and get my daughter in law and my granddaughter in this house!"

Daddy laughed, and I couldn't contain mine either. "Well, you heard her," he said, and I rose to my feet. He put his hand against my back and led me towards the house. "Daddy, Mama, this is Addie, my wife, and this is Eden."

Mama's eyes seemed to be floating along with unshed tears. "It's very nice to meet you both. Two more women in the house. My two girls have finally arrived."

Grandad Pete looked at me strangely and asked my name.

"My name is Ben." I said, taking in his thinned out frame and his glazed look. He was confused and he just sat on the rocker on the front porch and ignored me. The house looked exactly how I left it, the same yellow curtains, and tan colored furniture with green pillows, the same smell of vanilla. I could hear Addie and my mother gushing over Eden. Daddy looked over at me and smiled.

"You look beat up son."

I huffed. "Beat up doesn't begin to describe it."

"We need to celebrate," Mama said.

"That's a good idea," Daddy said.

I looked at them, my eyes wide. "You don't need to do all of that. I don't deserve it."

"You've been gone for seven years. A celebration is needed."

Addie smiled and I nodded. "Ok."

I turned my attention back to the large bay windows that overlooked the lake.

"Pa, Mama, may Addie and I be excused for just a moment, I want to take her down by the lake."

"Sure son, it gives us time to plan," Pa said, and Mama reached for Eden as Addie handed her over. "My goodness, she's a pretty little newborn. Ben you weren't this cute so early," Mama said, winking and shooing us out.

I grabbed Addie's hand and led her outside. "I love it already," Addie said, and I smiled back at her. We both approached the lake and I removed my shoes. "What are you doing?" she asked.

"We're going for a swim."

"We?"

"Yes, come on."

"Ben, we can't strip and swim in your parents home."

"You can leave the clothes on, just take off your shoes."

"This is crazy."

"Didn't you say walking was good? I'm sure swimming can't be much more dangerous."

She sighed. "Ok, I'm coming," she said, as she took off her shoes. We both held hands and approached the water's edge and dipped in. The water felt cold as it reached our knees, then hips, the shoulders. Then Addie kicked onto her back and began to float, and I followed suit. I closed my eyes and finally the tears ran down my face, falling diagonally across my cheeks into the lake.

"How do you feel?" I heard Addie call out to me.

"Clean," I called back.

Acknowledgements

Without the one who has made me clean, none of this would have been possible. God has made everything beautiful in its time.

A special thank you goes to my family who have stood by my side and supported my dreams. They've brainstormed with me on this novel, they've traveled with me to Idlewild. *Idle, Wild, Love* would have never been possible without you. Daddy, Mommy, and DJ, I love you.

To the Chaffer's and Rev. Deborah Elliot, you made traveling to Idlewild more than worthwhile. You made it feel like a second home.

To the 2013 Summer in the City staff and missions team, thank you for providing me with all the tours around the city for five weeks. We grew together over that time, and I needed you during that time to make this story real.

To my friends, Timothy, Darian, Raven, Kayla, Atara, Eboni, and Claudia thank you for listening to me rant on and on about this book. Thank you for contributing in whatever way you could, whether that was taking amazing photos of me so I could build my website, or just letting me cry out of stress and frustration when writer's block had claimed me. Ayana, thank you for your support and French translations and lessons.

To A. Manette Ansay, my teacher, my mentor, I have learned more about writing from you than I could've ever imagined. Thank you for helping me learn how to translate everything I see, feel, taste, touch and hear onto paper. You are amazing.

And last but not least, to all of my supporters on the web, at the Perrine New Testament Church of God, and the University of Miami, you made this process exciting. You made me realize that this novel was never about me. I am secondary. It was always about you all. I hope the messages from this book have touched you the same way it has touched me.

About the Author

Shaida Escoffery- Born in Brooklyn, NY, raised in Miami, FL was the recipient of the 2013 Atlantic Coast Conference Innovation and Creativity Fellowship for her writing at the University of Miami. She has been a student of the Creative Writing Department at the University of Miami for four years. Her first published novel promises to capture the hearts of readers.

www.ingramcontent.com/pod-product-compliance
Lightning Source LLC
Chambersburg PA
CBHW020107180626
46812CB00006B/2505